BLOOMERS

KELBY GUILFOYLE

Front Cover Design by Taylor Sterry
Back Cover Design by Kelby Guilfoyle

ISBN 978-1-8383125-0-3

Follow me on Instagram:

@kelbyguilfoyle
@thehumanprincess for weird and silly art stuff

Kelby Guilfoyle is a writer and creative from Ireland.

They would describe themselves as a madhouse-flower-princess with a streak of surreal fantasy-land charm. A college dropout turned playwright and author. Their work has been described as being MIND BLOWING, DREAMY and having a TRULY DISTINCT VOICE.

Their other work includes their debut novel *Poppy*. A memoir and avant-garde, half fictious tell all about a non-binary television actor turned new dad. Available wherever you buy books. (sorta).

Chapter 1.

The church bell rang as flocks of thirsty Christ-goers shuffled out onto the streets after Sunday mass. They had blurry faces, and they swayed as they walked. Pretty little daffodils dangling on the edge of a rockface. Flow got the scissors in her hands and started cutting out the left eye piece. I watched as she did it, keeping my other eye on the church cars, leaving the carpark. The bucket was painted an ice blue, with a few dodgy pink brushstrokes 'round the edges. She always looked angry when she was concentrated. She crudely cut the hole clear and circled her finger 'round the insides of it. She placed the bucket to the side and took out a lunchbox with the Virgin Mary skateboarding on it. She had a hemp flower 'cross her chest and she was flipping the bird. Inside were about twenty pre-rolled joints, all delicate and beautiful. She poked her fingers into the metal tin and pulled one out. Her nails were bitten down, and the varnish was all torn apart. She took it 'round her lips and sparked it with a dinky pink lighter. She looked at me, and I could see the sides of her lips poke up. She took the joint into her fingers and we both slipped the buckets over our faces. My eyes could see out the holes, in a single straight unhinged view. I could see the last few cars pull out of the church carpark. I peeled the pair of old swimming goggles over the bucket and they covered the eye sockets, almost too perfectly. I pulled the bucket and held it right above my nose. Flow passed me the joint and I took a huge inhale and dropped the bucket down and breathed out. The heat of the rising smoke and the suction of air forced sweat down my cheeks. I could barely see anything out of the fogged-up goggles. The bucket made everything muffled too, so I barely heard Flow, all I could hear was a sort of crying silence. I was at home in this dense void of hotboxed grass. I sat into it, I wanted to get away from myself and just let it take over. But as soon as it started to become peaceful, Flow would nudge me, and I would slip the bucket up again to take another hit. It went on like this for a few more minutes until the blunt was done with. We didn't say a single word. Going in and out of darkness and light was jarring, my eyes kept having to adjust, and it made everything hazier. I was submerged into the bucket, sleeping in this euphoria when I heard Flow pop open the metal tin and spark the second blunt. I waited for it to be my turn and I tried to adjust my eyes a bit to some semblance of light, but the shock of white when I pulled the bucket up, still remained. I took a pull of this second one and it hit the same as the first really, same weed, same sort of feeling, except now I was more dazed, I guess. I arose again, and I dug my fingers into the bucket and tried wiping the goggles clear, but it didn't help much, I could see the outlines of crude shapes for a few moments until they fogged up again. I dangled my feet 'round over the edge of the billboard we were sitting on. The image of a honey crunch cereal bar was plastered behind us. I found Flow's legs and I kicked against them, she kicked back. It was the first real connection we had since we began. I turned my head to face hers and I am pretty sure she did the same, I couldn't quite make it out of course, but it just felt like she did. She nudged me and I popped up from the bucket, this time slipping it off completely to scratch the top of my head. I took a puff and this time I didn't put the bucket back on. I was well and truly baked. I looked down below, at my feet dangling, at Flow's feet, at the small branches of trees, at the cars whizzing by. I poked up and I watched as Flow sat with the bucket on her head. Her bucket was painted red with some yellow marks on it. She was looking up at the sky, I took another inhale of smoke and watched her stare into the heavens. I quenched the dead blunt and waved my fingers up and down my palms. I watched at where she was looking, forgetting that she couldn't probably see anything at all, inside that bucket. The sky was an orange glow, a few clouds whisked 'round and the black bodies of crows painted the blue and white, as they flew in circles. I looked back down after a few moments and I watched as Flow crawled back to the world and pulled off the bucket. She glared at me but didn't stay on my eyes for too long, it was a morsel of a second. She caught hold of the metal tin once more, this time admiring the painting of the Virgin Mary before digging her fist in to scoop out another burning stick. She looked down at the lunchbox and I could see the tips of her lips begin to bend upwards.

"The Virgin Mary is a ride" she said
She began to laugh; it was a full and honest laugh. Her nostrils spat out and her teeth sharpened wide inside her mouth, as her tongue did a ballerina's dance. She looked at me, wide mouthed and still laughing. She stopped and she entered another universe that lived inside of my eyes, it was this blooming carnival. She pursed her lips together, leaving this tiny gap in 'em. I leant into that crevice between her lips. I felt safe

looking at it. She ran her pinkie finger up the piece of skin that connected my index and my thumb. She stopped just shy of my wrist and held it still there, not applying pressure. I moved my eyes upwards towards her nose, still too scared to see her gaze. I could feel the rush of the breeze hit my chest. I could feel this heavy avalanche happening inside of me. I was flaming up. I let out this hot air breath, it made a hushed rustling noise. I watched as her nose ring swayed. Her nostrils were small and cute. Flow plopped the third blunt in the small gap in her lips and blazed it up, taking a longer than usual pull, she turned to the side and blew the air out. She took her pinkie up and scratched her nose. She passed me the stick and I inhaled, and I suffocated myself back into the bucket. I coughed the smoke out into the plastic sides, and it rose up and all 'round. I couldn't see anything. I crossed my fingers into one another, and I wiped where her pinkie was with my thumb. We sat and we smoked another blunt before we hit a block. The metal ladder that hung out from the billboard seemed deadly enough sober, but it was a hellish madness, at this all-time bake. We decided to just sit and let the crumble wear off for a few hours. Flow laid down with the bottoms of her converse facing me. The left shoe had some pink gum on it and the right was clean. I slumped against the edge of the honey crunch billboard. It was a tiring silence up there, I wanted to say something to her, but it was as if I forgot how to speak. My lips did all the movements, but nothing came out. I think I manged a sigh, but I'm not sure she even heard it. A few hours ticked on and eventually I could feel myself starting to come down off the high. Flow was asleep, I leant over her and watched a moment before nudging her up.

"We better head down before it gets too dark" I whispered out loud

I climbed down the white painted metal ladder first, it wobbled in the wind. I got half-way down when Flow started descending. We eventually both hit soil and the ground air felt good against my cheeks. We both stood looking at each other for a moment, cars zooming by. It was this intense haze. I caught her eyes for the first real time that day. She had this stare, and her eyes, they were these gorgeous brown cookies. I sucked my lips inwards and licked the edges of them. The folds of her lips turned up yet again as she smiled wide, as if her mouth were a river bend.

"Happy birthday Harper" she said
We both walked separate ways and I really tried not to look back at her, but I couldn't help it, I turned 'round

and I noticed that she too was flashing her eyes at me. We both stood nearly twenty feet apart, looking at one another. Even from that far away, I could still feel her gaze. "I want to run to her" I kept saying it in my head. Over and over, I kept saying it. "I want to run to her", the words started to merge together, it became this chanting biblical creed that I kept washing 'round my head. But we both just stood there. The cars zoomed past and the night sunk down. She smiled at me, this time it held a sliver of pain within it. She turned around and walked away. I stood still in the night-time glow of that street watching her sway, she was this dollish flower, a daffodil flowing against the edge of a cliff. I turned around and I walked away too. This time I didn't look back, I just kept walking.

Chapter 2.

The candles were all wonky donkey, shovelled into the cake last minute. It had purple icing and a cream squeezed message that read: Happy Birthday Harper. The embers of the flaming candles burnt orange 'cross my face. I took a deep breath and I made a wish. I blew the candles out. My mum and dad cheered and clapped, as if I had cured cancer. I watched as my mum re-lit the candles and got me to blow 'em out again, but this time for a photo; which she could then use to boaster her love for her daughter online. Her Facebook profile was full of half blurred pictures of our dog Patch and selfies of herself suppling wine. The cake was sliced up and plated out, and it wasn't half bad. They looked right through me, almost inside of me. Two pairs of peering parent eyes. I wiped some fresh cream from my upper lip and smiled an obvious fake smile, but I felt compelled to at least give them something.

"My girl, all grown up" dad spat some cake onto the silver plate in front of his fat face
I blew some air out my nose and pretended to laugh. I was seventeen, hardly a grown up. Mum tipped some

more wine into her mug, she liked to pretend she wasn't an alkie by using a mug instead of a glass, she was beyond the world's intelligence sometimes. I wobbled my plate against the uneven bumpy table, watching the edges lift and see-saw back and forth. Dad had this huge smile on him. It was this devilish menace. I indulged him by smiling back. He pushed out his chair and went off, a grin on his cheeks. When he came back, he held a gift bag with a cute ribbon in his hands. He placed it on the table and pushed it towards me.

"It's just something small" he said
I pulled the ribbon apart and folded out some of the cushioning coloured paper. Mum sipped her wine as I peered into the bag. There was a dainty box inside. I clicked it open and it was a pair of earrings, big blue flower earrings. They were beautiful. They were partly worn, with some slight rusting.

"They were your nan's" mum said, coming up from her mug
I took out my hoops and I placed them on, they had a weight to 'em, you could really feel it, but I liked that. I smiled again, but this time is wasn't pretend, this time it was for real.

Crumpling against the silk sheets of my bed, I

kicked my foot up the wall, squishing my toes against the cold plasterboard. I pretended I was walking up the walls. I cocked my neck back and swung my head towards the end of my room. My back arching upwards and my pelvis holding the weight. I looked at the pale nothing at the end of my room. There were a few odd socks thrown 'round the floor and a curling iron, with the wire tangling over itself, laying by a few schoolbooks. I cupped my tit and began to squish it 'round my fingers to try feel something. I thought maybe I was crazy, everyone would talk about feeling themselves, but I had never tried it. Flow loved to go on about it, how it was a woman's euphoric right to pleasure herself, I just found it a bit icky and kind of gross. I stared down at my crotch; I was wearing a simple white pair of underwear. My legs were badly shaven, I could still see a few hairs sticking out. I fiddled my fingers 'round against the silk patterns, slowly moving downwards with each ticking second. I caught my fingers on the edge of my underwear and pulled down. My vagina screamed at me, it looked alive. I had a patch of hair, a brown splatter of dirt. My heart was beating way faster than usual, I could feel every pump. I squeezed my eyelids shut and I took my index finger down. It was kind of similar to sticking your finger into a tub of petroleum jelly for the first time, you had all these ideas of what it might feel like, but then when you actually dug right down and into it, it was exactly what you imagined it to be, and also nothing like what you imagined it to be, all at the same time. I slowly found myself adjusting to it, I could feel the heaviness of my short exhales of breath wrapping 'round my face. A faint noise slid out from the gap of my front teeth. My door thumped and my dad called out to see if he could come in. I jumped up and quickly found my underwear and slipped it back on and grabbed a pair of pants from my press and pulled them right up, forgetting to do the buttons.

"Come in" I was out of breath

"You okay?" he would always ask, but this time I could feel the weight of it so much more

"I am fine" I turned my head away from his

"I just worry, that's all"

I choose not to reply, I just turned and looked at him. He placed his hand on my shoulder, and the weight of his fingers almost left an imprint. He sat there for a moment before lifting his hand off and walking back out. I fell onto my bed and sighed. My phone lit up in that awful blue hue, and I reached my arm out and fondled it up into my hand. It was a photo message of a guy I had been talking to online, his name was Goose. He was holding his dick in his hand and his feet were pressed into the tiles of his bathroom. I folded up my top and took a picture of my tits and sent it to him. I dropped my phone on the bed and I stared back down at my crotch, and I noticed the buttons of my jeans were all opened and the white of my underwear was showing.

Chapter 3.

Goose rolled a fat cig and swivelled it 'round. He took a drag, and then he looked at me. He had this brush of ginger hair, and this solid rock-type face. He had these crude cheekbones, that were chiselled into place.

"You got decent tits" he took a puff of smoke

"Thanks" I curled my hair 'round my finger

"Want to maybe see a movie?"

"Sure"

He got up and walked over to another wall, it was obvious a few of the lads were eyeing his every move. They chuckled at him as he sat down.

"How does he know what your tits look like?" Flow coughed the words out

"I sent him a picture"

"Why?"

"I dunno, just did"

She slumped into herself and spooned up some of her yoghurt with her lollipop. She was different than the rest of us, she didn't care about the things we cared about. She was this firesome soul; I don't think anything had ever hurt her. She drew these white freckles onto her face one time in maths, and with her black skin, they really popped out. She had used tip-ex to do it and the teacher sent her to the principal's office, and she got detention for three weeks. I thought it was far too long a sentence, until she told me later that she called the principal "a fat fuck". Then it felt too short of a sentence. I watched as she stuck her lollipop into her yoghurt, licking it off and dunking it in again, she kept doing it for a while until I spoke up.

"He's kind of cute" I said

"He's a fucking gargoyle"

"Can you not be happy for me?"

She sighed and she opened her lips to smile at me. It looked very weird and made me uncomfortable. She started making all kinds of silly and obtuse faces, squirming 'round, standing up on the wall and making strange noises.

"I am happy for you, my dear" she spoke out her nostrils, pretending to be a witch

I just laughed at her, and she laughed at me laughing at her, we both laughed together. She was the only person who could really make me laugh, she was all I had that was good in this world. I think she knew it too, just by the look of her face sometimes. The sun drooled down on her prettiness as she twirled her feet 'round and danced on that wall. She was everything in that moment, magical and dreamlike. Some of the other fools laughed at her, they thought she was mental, and maybe she was, but she didn't care.

Flow sat playing her *Gameboy* as I tried on some dresses. A blue one with white buttons, she glanced up and she cackled before returning to her game. I took it off and stood in my bra and underwear. My feet were small, and I had these skinny toes. I looked at myself in the mirror, at all the crooked jars of my body. I found my eyes at Flow, who was watching my back, glimpsing at my half-nude body.

"What about this yellow one?" I pointed

"Yeah" she poured down and into her knees
I slipped my feet into the yellow dress. It had this flowing seam, it was beautiful. Flow had this tight clench on her lips, as if she was holding something back. Words were locked in her mouth, and she was washing them back down into herself with her tongue. She finally opened them, and she seemed happier, in a strange kind of way.

"You look..." she tried gathering her words
I watched as she rocked her body about, almost beating herself up.

"The yellow one then" I smiled at her
Suddenly, my cheeks were wet, and tears were flowing

down my face. I wiped them away, but in reality, my eyes were as dry as a hot desert. I was having a surreal fever dream again. Flow was playing her game, and I didn't know what was true, and what had happened, but I knew something wasn't quite right.

Goose had this green pick-up truck; it had these big black wheels and was covered in rust and mud and dirt. He had a penis shaped air freshener, and his left seat was all pulled apart by a dog. I sat there in my yellow dress, and he parked up the car, a bit too far away from the screen, but I could still see it. It was one of them outdoor cinema things, I had never been, there weren't many cars there, maybe four or five. The ignition stopped and he sniffed his nose in and gawked at me, eyes of pure flame.

"So?" he salivated at my tits

"So, what?"

"So, so…" he bit his lower lip with his teeth

"Can we at least wait for the movie to start?"

Okay, I should explain. I have never had sex before, not even a little bit. I kissed a guy once for maybe a minute, and that was nice, but I don't really remember it. And it's just everyone keeps talking about their orgasms and their vaginas and how it feels so good and how you should try it, and Goose was this big hunk of man, with eyes and ears and stuff. I didn't feel anything around him, people say you get wet before you do anything, but I was dry, I mean, I think I was dry, I couldn't really tell. We had this thing planned out between us, he messaged me the night before saying, 'Is sex on the cards, or what?' I thought it was forward, but I thought, now's my chance, yanno, I should take it. So, I took a picture of my bits and I said 'yeah, sex is on the cards, sex is all the cards, the cards are sex cards'. He sent me a video of him masturbating, I didn't watch it. I clicked off the minute I saw it, the thought of him, inside of me, made me feel terribly sick.

The movie was this black and white classic, about a woman who wanted to marry this younger man. I couldn't hear a word of it, but it had subtitles. I don't think he watched a second of it, he had his eyes locked on me the whole time. I watched as the woman took the young uneducated man in her arms, and I read the subtitles underneath. *'Your body changes me'*. I reached over and put my hand on his cheek, and I kissed him, the white lights creating shadows out of our moving faces. It felt different from my first kiss, this was more real. I pulled out and my heart was racing, what the hell was I doing?

"Okay, okay, let's do it" I grabbed him

He pulled up that yellow dress and he got his fingers to me, it felt incredible, my body ached, and a shiver climbed up my spine. I clenched my eyes closed and I thought about Flow. Goose didn't even exist in my mind; all I could think about was her. This time it wasn't a dream, this time it was real. I opened my eyes and found the movie, as he kept going. I watched as the mother of the woman asked her daughter *'What do you want?',* the woman sat still a moment before she replied. Goose pulled my attention and grabbed my left tit in his grubby hand.

"Are you okay?" he pressed against my face

"I am so sorry" I clicked open the door

I ran through the fields, away from that place. I almost stumbled through everything; I was that much in a haze. The streetlamps were all orange and beautiful and I stood under one for a moment, took out a joint and a lighter that Flow had given me, I sparked it and took a pull. I smoked into the night air, into the whirlwind 'round me. *'What do you want?',* the woman smiled, and she said, *'I want to feel something'.* I smoked under that lamp and I walked home. I climbed onto the roof and into the window of my room. I slipped out of the dress and stood in my bra and underwear, looking at myself in the mirror. I started to dance, squishing my toes between the floorboards. I fell onto my bed and I looked down at my crotch, I moved my hand down and tore off my underwear and I started thinking about Flow, I imagined her body beside mine, I imagined all of it, I imagined everything.

Chapter 4.

It must have been the windiest day ever recorded. I stood outside the schoolyard sipping my juice-box and waddling my feet over the number three in this jangly made, horribly chalked, crudely doodled hopscotch. My blonde locks played airplane in the wind. Some hairs got caught in my teeth and I could barely see from the constant blow. I turned the white straw over in my teeth. I bit the tip of it and tried squeezing the juice up, to see if it'd fit through. It got caught by the clench of my teeth, but I kept trying. I barely remember it, I kind of blurred these parts out of my brain. But I remember the wind, I remember that. She stood and she looked at me, with those same gorgeous-hazelnut-chocolate-box-eyes of hers.

"What're you doing?" she said

"Hopscotch" I replied

She started hopscotching, counting the numbers out loud. I moved out of her way and watched as she got to the end. She kept going back and forth until she stopped, and gave me this big, almost sinister stare.

"My name's Flow, we are friends now"

"Okay" Imagine, that's how easy it was

She had me, the minute she saw me, I was part of her. We would spend every living minute together; we were there through all of it. It was our last week of sixth class when Flow's dad died. I remember she said a few words at the funeral, they weren't her own, they were words from the bible, but still, they made me cry. She didn't cry at all, she just stayed stone faced through all of it, now that I think of it, I don't think I have ever seen her cry. I only found out a few days after the funeral that her dad had killed himself; Flow found him hanging, he had used his scarf to do it.

At the funeral there were all types of sandwiches, tuna, chicken and mayo, chicken without mayo, chicken with bacon, turkey, ham and cheese, egg salad, ham and turkey. It was a real feast of triangular sandwiches. We must have been around 14 at this stage, yeah, I think so. I stood in the function room, in the middle of all her family, sipping away at my juice-box; I would bring a juice-box everywhere, even my best-friend's dad's funeral. Flow poured her eyes at me from across the room, she was shaking hands with some of her dad's friends. She shook her head at me; she hated when I would drink from my juice-boxes. I love the noise at the end of a juice-box, it's one of my favourite sounds. She thought I looked like a baby when I drank out of one, which I couldn't ever understand. Babies didn't drink juice-boxes, they drank bottles. This whole shaking hands and pretending to understand the weight of death continued for maybe another 2 hours. Flow hated it. She broke away with a pack of her mother's cigarettes, catching me by the hands and waltzing out the door.

"Where'd you get those?"

"Do you want one, or not?"

I stopped asking questions and we both smoked in this field by the function hall. The function hall was the old sports centre, it had a room in the back for parties and funerals. This day was a very calm day, maybe the calmest day in all existence. We shared the cigs between us both, she got 8 and I got 7, it was only fair, she had just lost her dad.

"How do you feel?"

"Like a dead flower that someone is constantly trying to water" she darted her eyes at the clouds in the sky, she watched their every single move

"Yeah..." I didn't really know what to say

I stood up and I took a stick from the ground and started engraving into the muck. A make-shift hopscotch, with all the numbers and everything. I started hopscotching, and she looked at me whilst I did. She smiled, it was as if I had broken into her heart, as if a drop of water finally made her move, as if the dying flower had some life.

The bright pink nail varnish drooled onto the dresser. I jolted to wipe it clean, but I ended up knocking over the jar and spilling a puddle out, and it dripped slowly down onto the floorboards. I didn't even try to clean it, I just watched it drip. I was still getting used to make-up, I didn't usually wear it, but this was a special night, so I wanted to go all out, I wanted her to notice me. My nail varnish application skills were average at best, I couldn't keep the polish from getting on my skin, and so it was splattered desperately 'cross my fingertips. I wore my good bra, the bra with extra padding to make my chest look bigger; *size is power*. I read that in a girly mag one time, so it must have been true. I also read that Zac Efron likes to get his chest waxed at a circus by dancing girls in purple bikinis, so who knows what is true these days. Laid out on my bed was a dress my mum wore when she was my age, when she first danced with my dad. It was this perfect red dress. I had these black sparkled Doc Marten's to go with it, and I never really let my hair down, but tonight, I decided to let it free. I applied some red lipstick and I could hear the beeping horn of Flow's rusty car. I zipped up the dress and tied the laces on my boots and walked out the door. She was smoking out the window, she had extreme black eyeshadow and had drawn white freckles on her face. She only ever really wore black, but tonight she was wearing this beautiful white gown. She looked like heaven.

"Tip-ex?"

"I thought, why the fuck not"

"You really want to piss 'em off, don't you?"

"No" she said with a cheeky grin on her face

The graduation ball, a beautiful mess of people with no clue of who they are, or what they want. And the worst of it all, there was non-alcoholic punch. You only ever see punch in the movies. Of course, don't you worry, Flow had us covered. She managed to smuggle a shoulder of vodka through. She poured some into the plastic cups and gave me one, and she knocked hers back clean and I had to follow, she could make me do anything, so I did. My face squished in and my eyes watered. She grabbed my hand and pulled me onto the dancefloor. My heart was exploding. She flung her arms about and she danced like crazy. I only barely moved myself 'round, just enough to not look like I was standing still. She slowed down and she opened her eyes, she grabbed me closer to her. I could feel her breath now. My armpits were stained with sweat at this point. She was electric and I was this damaged vase, a place for her flower to grow in.

"How was your date?" she softly spoke

"I ran away"

"You ran away?"

"He wasn't what I wanted"

"What do you want?"

I looked up at her melting eyes. I began to speak but she got there before me, which made my heart thump louder and more viciously.

"I need to tell you something Harper"

"Yeah?" My heart stopped beating

If the world had been burning for so long, and the fires were dark and deadly. And houses were burnt to the ground, and people blazed into ash on the sidewalks. Birds falling from the skies because of heat-stroke. This moment right now, it felt like the very first rainfall. I didn't know how to describe it, but it felt so new, and so fresh, and it seemed to calm the burning fires. The melting butter of her brown eyes spilled onto mine, as I sunk into her. I waited for her words to fall out.

"I..." she started to speak

Fuck it. I couldn't wait, I leant in and I held her face and kissed her. I could feel everyone's eyes looking at us, thousands of raw eyes. I pushed back, and my lips squelched as they pressed off hers. She just looked at me. A bunch of boys beside her started calling her and me 'lesbians', and I could see her face turning by this. She spun 'round and kicked one of 'em in the balls and punched another in the face. The principal screamed over and pulled her off another boy, and she was grabbed and dragged out through the hall of laughing faces. I ran across the room and I stood on the table with the fake punch and ignited my lighter, and the flame took hold and the sprinklers all started to rain down. I watched her being dragged through the hall, the rain pouring down, people drenched in water. She was drowning and I didn't know if she was crying or if she was just wet, but she smiled at me, and I just knew that everything was going to be okay.

Chapter 5.

I got sent home after I rained on the party. And the next day I found myself sitting inside the principal's office. He had the fattest-pumpkin-face I had ever seen. His hands were smudged into his desk, they crushed down so hard that I could see the multitude of folds and wrinkles.

"Harper, why did you turn on the sprinklers?"

"I dunno"

He sighed, as he probably always did when a student ended up in his room. He had a soft spot for me, ever since the incident. He was the one who found us.

"I have to do my job Harper"

"I know"

He left me off with a warning, and I was on my way. I walked down the street, with the cars zooming by me. I had a yellow schoolbag and white socks up to my knee. When I got home, mum was arguing with dad about where to position the egg cups. Mum insisted they go in the cutlery drawer, which dad thought was barbaric.

"Egg cups aren't cutlery" he said

Dad thought they'd work better on the counter-top,

by the bowl of eggs.

"Right where you can grab 'em" he muttered

"I don't want to see 'em everyday" she had a face on her, like she was chewing a wasp

"It's best to keep the egg stuff, with the eggs"
I walked upstairs and slumped my bag on the floor. Climbed my sweaty knees onto my bed and kicked off my shoes and pulled down the left sock, slowly. My nose crunched up and my eyes watered as I did it. A fresh cut was painted red, right under my knee. I took both the socks fully off, and I flung my head back and closed my eyes. The egg cup war raged on downstairs and my ears were beginning to bleed, so I turned my music up loud and I locked my door. I was safe in my black cave. I frowned down at the fresh cut once more and I thought, well, maybe not that safe.

Don't use scissors, they create this messy and deep wound. The best thing to use is the small blade off a pencil sharpener, easy to hide, and easy to find. Don't just go right into it either, make sure the thing is well cleaned and disinfected, you don't want any nasty infections, they'll be way too hard to hide. Don't go too deep, especially if it's your first time, there's no need to hurt yourself that much. You can always get deeper if needed. Start slow, there's no rush. Water is your best friend, make sure to wash down your wounds with warm water, not too hot or not too cold. I keep a packet of mermaid band-aids under my bed, you can buy all different types of band-aids, or if the cut gets way out of hand, you can always try cover it another way, long sleeve tops, knee high socks, the list is endless, be creative. Don't let it become an addiction, it's so easy to get addicted to things these days, don't you think? We all feel like dirt under a burning radiator, madly depressed and savagely displaced. We all cope differently, some people drink, some people do drugs and others cut themselves. I do all those things, because I am fucking fabulous. And don't start with 'There's always someone to talk to' or 'What about a councillor?' because, I am not stupid. I talk about it a lot, with my councillor.

"You can't just post online about *How to Safely Self Harm*, Harper!" said Teddy, my councillor

"I thought it would help someone"

"You can't just promote it"

"I wasn't. I just thought if people were going to do it, and people were going to do it, then wouldn't it have been best if they did it safely?"

"You're glorifying it again Harper"

He fiddled his pen 'round the paper, writing notes

'HARPER IS INSANE' et cetera. I just sat there and waited for him to speak again.

"So, tell me about this new cut?" he said

"Well, it happened 2 nights ago"

"Okay, and why did you do it?"

The water rained down, quenching the flame of my lighter. Miss Salamander (because she looked like a lizard and I can't remember her real name) grabbed me down from the table, knocking the fake punch in the process. She phoned my parents, while I waited in an empty classroom. I didn't know where Flow had gone. I dreamt of her tapping on the window and both of us escaping into the night, but she never came. It felt super strange being in that classroom all alone, just waiting for my parents to arrive. I could faintly hear the music from the school gym, it echoed 'round the place. This is what it must feel like getting kicked out of a night-club, I thought to myself. I could see the illumination of lights shine through the window, and I got up to check the damage. It was Flow's mum, she got out of the car and a few minutes later pulled Flow by the arm and shoved her in, it was as if she was being arrested. I could still smell her perfume on my chest, and the taste of her raspberry lip balm on my mouth. I blew 'gainst the window glass and in the condensation, I drew a love heart with my finger. The lights in the classroom frazzled, and suddenly all blew out. A black tar dripped from the bulbs and onto the floor. The love heart faded.

When I got home, I went straight to my room. If you have ever had the best night of your life, and all of a sudden you were standing in the middle of your room, so disconnected and away from it all, that it didn't even feel real, that somewhere another reality had exploded and this one took over, then you'll understand why I did it. I just went into a place that I couldn't escape from. My mind went purple and I got the blade and sliced right under my knee, I couldn't feel myself and so by accident I went way too deep, and the blood started spilling everywhere. I wiped the floor with an old t-shirt and ran out my room and into the bathroom to clean it off. I wasn't going to be able to hide this one with a band-aid, I thought to myself, as I was coming down from the burning high. It's not that I like cutting myself, it's just I do it. I can't really explain it, I just sort of shut off. Even then, the best night of my life, I was bleeding on the tiles of my bathroom floor, all alone and with nowhere to go.

I didn't tell him about the kiss, or about Flow. I had never said the words out loud. As the week ticked on, I ate my lunch alone and I waited for her to text me back, but I assumed she had her phone taken off her, and she must have got expelled for a week, I thought to myself. It was weird being in that school without her. Everyone looked at me different, some people called me names, others just walked away from me. I wasn't well, but the blade took her place for the week, which I know isn't a good thing, but I wouldn't have done it if I didn't need to. We would both laugh about it, she'd ask why I do it, and everything would be okay, we made a promise, out in that field the day of her dad's funeral.

She said "I need you"

"We need each other"

"Don't ever leave me Harper, please"

"I can't, I'm your sun, wherever you grow, I'll be at the other end, no matter what"

"Promise me"

"I promise"

The school bell rang, and I was off to my next class. It was the same classroom where I had last seen her, just outside that window. I didn't hear a single word of that class, I waited for her to tap on the glass, and for her to save me, but she never did.

Chapter 6.

Hello, my name is Larry and I am a joint and I live inside a metal lunchbox. It's a beautiful little place, it's uh, perfect for a joint like me. I was rolled about three weeks ago; nobody has opened the box since the day atop the billboard; that's where we lost The Three Gary's and little Susie Wan. To be smoked is the dream, chocked in those slim fingers, pushed into the mouth and puffed away. A joint wants to be sparked and inhaled. It's what we were born to do. A few dust bites have joined us in the last few weeks, they are all right, they keep to themselves. What have I been doing to pass the time, yeah...that's a good question. A few of the guys have resorted to praying, it's kind of a cult really.

"It's a religion" says a joint in the corner who is on his knees praying to something sinister

"A way of life" says another

I just kind of go about my day really, there's this joint that I have been talking to recently, she's pretty darn cool. Her name is Marigold. She's wrapped up with good papers too, looks pretty good in 'em. She has this incredible twist; it's all the guys have been talking about, they just won't shut up about it.

"Marigold. She's a twister" says Barry, a joint who is squeezing milk out of a dust mite cow

"She's definitely got this awesome twist down there, she uh, she knows it too" says another

"I'd smoke the shit out of her" they all say
I got this bit of weed hanging out from me, I don't want to poke it out because it might drain me, you got to be careful, you can't just go pulling at things. I think she likes it; she hasn't said anything about it, but I see her looking at it, it's quite a look really. She's got these beautiful eyes, like uh, perfect.

"Larry, he's nice...did he really say that he liked me?" Marigold says blushing

Living inside a lunchbox isn't luxury, but you got to remember, we are all just joints, we aren't used to much. Terry lived inside the front pocket of a schoolbag for five months, tell 'em Terry.

"Back of schoolbag, that was Terry"
Terry has been here the longest, poor fella never gets picked, uh, it's a lucky bag, I don't think the humans know what they are doing when they stick their hands in, it's just all potluck really. I have decided that today I'm going to ask Marigold on a date, you know, I think she's going to say yes. I just got to go for it, I mean,

what can I lose, you know. I just must do it. I got her dust mite milk, I seen her drinking some, I think she likes it. Just like a gift, something to say hi with. Look, there she is, just sitting down by the holy dent. I am going to do it, wish me luck.

"Marigold, I got you some dust mite milk"

"Larry, that's nice" she takes the milk

"The holy dent" I point at it

"Yeah, that's what they say"

"If you look at it long enough, it uh…"

"The lunchbox opens, I know the story"

"Yeah. I like your papers by the way"

"I like your bit of weed" she looks at it

"Oh, I seen you looking" I awkwardly say

"Yeah, was I? Sorry"

"Marigold, I was thinking…"

"Yeah?"

"Would you maybe, sometime…"

"I'd love to, you mean a date, right?"

"Yeah, right" I laugh

"Yeah, I'd uh, that'd be nice" she laughs

"See you tonight?"

"See you tonight" she smiles at me

"Okay" I walk away from her

Did you see that? She said yes. We are going on a date,

tonight. She liked the milk too, I think it was good to start with it, you know, it set things up nicely.

Okay, so here I am, waiting here outside the inside trademark. It's a fancy little spot, I thought it'd be nice. I got here a bit early, I couldn't really think all day, I was in my head. All the guys wished me luck, which was nice, they are okay, you know. We have all been through the worst together. It's a family, it's good. Marigold, she's amazing, I think she could be the one. I really do. Do you hear that noise, it's kind of loud? Holy fuck. What's going on here, as you can see, from all the tumbling 'round and stuff, we have been picked up and we are on the move. This is the first tumbling in weeks, means it's smoke time. I didn't uh, I didn't plan for this. It's good, it's uh, no, it's, yeah, it's good. Means a few of us will get smoked, which is why we exist, so it kind of makes sense. I better go find Marigold, make sure she's okay. Probably must reschedule the date and all, with the rumblings going on. She's always by the dent, so I better check there first, see if she's there, it's going to be good.

"Marigold, there you are, by the dent"

"Larry, it's happening" she looks sad

"I know" I look at her, she looks beautiful

"What does it feel like?" she stares at the dent

"Barry got lit before, said it uh, he said it's wonderful, it's what we were born to do Marigold"

"I know, but what about us?"

"There will always be us, even after all this"

"I am scared"

"It's going to be okay, no matter what happens, we go out like a light, together"

"Hold me"

"Always" I hold my hands 'round her and squeeze, I can feel every part of her, all my world begins to happen in that embrace, everything starts to make sense

Flow opens the metal lunchbox and digs her hands in and pulls out two joints, they both seem to be clinging onto one another, she must pull them apart almost. She keeps the one with a bit of weed sticking out and hands the other one to Harper. They both smoke in that same spot, watching the church bells ring and the people climbing into their cars. It's just another tired Sunday afternoon. It's the first time they have seen each other in a few weeks. Flow grabs her bucket and begins to place it on her head, but Harper reaches out and stops her. They don't need the buckets no more, because getting high wasn't why they were here. They locked eyes, and the two joints, each in their respective hands, seemed to almost look at one another, and for a moment, everything was still.

Chapter 7.

Flow was anything but easy to describe, she was this floating enigma that vomited buttercup star ships out of her ass. Every time you thought you understood something, she'd break it right open and leave you speechless. Flow was short for Flower, and Flower was short for Flower Princess and Flower Princess was short for What the fuck is a Flower Princess? We smoke weed every Sunday on top of a billboard by the church; we told our parents we were volunteering to feed the priests and wash their fancy cars. We started a few weeks after Flow's dad died, she got this bag of weed from her cousin; who went to jail for dealing two months later. And, we decided to make it our little thing, I even bought her a Virgin Mary lunchbox to house the joints, which I thought was a killer present. Every week the billboard would change, *Terrence's Car Parts*, *Fruity Hoops and Chocolate Chunks*, and *Crocodile Energy Drink*. We would purposely not look at it during the week, so when Sunday came along, it would be this big surprise.

It was the week of Flow's 16th birthday, and we hadn't looked at the billboard all week, and we waged our bets, as per usual, she said "*Alcohol*", which was a pretty solid bet, I went with "*I think it'll be something worth seeing*". When we got up there and finally looked at it, in all its glaring glory. It was this beautiful mural, of all these flowers, and rainbows, and in the middle of it all was this princess, and she was black, with a crown on her head, made of pure white gold. She said she wanted something small. It took me all week, I painted it during the nights, I would climb out of my window, tape my phone to my face and splatter it on, bit by bit, all in my back garden, it was the only place big enough. I bought this huge sheet of plasterboard, the guy at the store said it would fit perfectly. I made sure to get there before she did on Sunday, I had this altar boy who I saw at church that day help me hoist it, I paid him what was left of my wallet. I robbed my dad's power drill and I screwed it in.

"Happy Birthday" I held her hand

"You did this for me?"

"You said you were a dead flower, but you never were, you are more alive than anyone, you're a flower princess"

"What the fuck is a flower princess?"

We climbed up the shaky ladder and smoked, birthday joints on the top of the world.

ARE YOU HAPPY? is plastered on the billboard. A phone number for a counselling service underneath. Just my luck, the billboard is mocking me, and it's our first time up here in about a month. My first-time seeing Flow again, since we first kissed. I see the waddle of feet, her familiar black boots. She has this diamond ring on her left pinkie, and the handle of the lunchbox slides up and down her palm. She stops in front of me and holds her hands out and nods her head, as if to say, *"yes, it is me"*.

"I could murder a joint right now" she says

"Same"

She holds the bottom rung of the ladder and before she climbs, whilst looking up towards the billboard, she stops a second.

"I am sorry..."

My lips slowly open, it takes a few seconds, but I finally get the courage to speak up, and in this heavy breathy voice, it comes out.

"For what?"

"All of it" she started climbing the ladder

I stood and watched her climb up, my heart was still, I could barely hear it. I grabbed hold of the metal bars, and I started climbing. We smoked and watched the world tip over, I held her in my arms, and I kissed her.

I won't lie, in that moment, I understood everything. I didn't have any worries, or any questions, or any concerns or anything. I was just there to exist, and I did. I really did. The night gathered on us quickly, although time was this made up thing, it merely just happened in front of us. She wrapped her fingers over my arms and pulled them off her body. She looked deathly and haunted.

"Harper, this isn't me…"
Everything she said blurred into this mess of words. It was the first time I had ever seen her cry.

"…I can't do this"
My heart sank. I wanted to jump off that billboard and splash my body on the flowers underneath. I hated that she played me, but the wash on her face, the mad drooping blush, it was clear as day, she wanted more. A dying flower can't see the sun, so it withers to nothing, falling petals, she was pushing me away, 'cus she knew what it was like to really lose, I could see it in her eyes, she wanted so badly to save me. But all I wanted was her. But maybe she didn't want me.

Her eyes were merry-go-rounds and her pupils were dashing horses. I saw a torn black spot drool from her eyelid. A gloopy slime juiced blackness. It dripped from her lid like rainwater. It grew into a puddle and it shook, and it tried forming. But the inky globular mess was too slippery to take any real shape. She didn't seem to notice, but my eyes were hardwired on the beast. I stuck my finger into the blob and circled 'round. That's when I noticed two small white pupils. It had eyes, and it was alive. I took two fingers and squished one of the white eyes, and clear puss squeezed onto my face and into my eyes. What was this monster, and why was it living inside of Flow? She glanced at me, and when she did, the ink vanished.

Chapter 8.

I dreamt about us touching each other last night. She was my best friend and I was in love with her, but she didn't love me back. I became so overwhelmed in my own falsified story, that I painted it all in rainbows. Everything made sense from my point of view, but most of that was all a bubble, this magnified bubble that was suffocating me. She let me kiss her; she kissed me back. I should have just fucked Goose and called it my life, that would've hurt less. In a way this was good, now I had something to point to, that would explain my crippling and painful sadness. I would be heartbroken, people would comfort me, and they'd say, 'I'm so sorry Harper, that sucks.' This is what I needed. I could listen to *Radiohead* now, and eat Ice-Cream and cry at old people holding hands at the park. I could start a blog called '*Suicide Lover*', and I could tell girls that it's okay if your crotch is dry and your tits are barely big enough to hug in your hand, you can always just slice up your wrist and kill yourself. There was a silver lining, shining down the side of my blade. And it helped me breath better. Everything would be okay; I could watch countless dickheads get to mutate her into their sick and perverted fantasies. I could watch their smiles cut her face into millions of particles, and I could watch those particles burst 'round the atmosphere and form tiny pockets of cancerous nightmares. And now every time I see her, I will constantly have this burning image of her body getting thrown around her room by some cock hole with a hard on. Do you want to know the saddest part of it all, it's that I thought I had a chance at love, that maybe for once in my life, something could just work out. You want to know what really pissed me off, is that after she tore my heart out, I went home and I cried for four hours, to be greeted not long after by my fucking period!

The doctor held my left breast in his hand, and he wobbled it about for a bit, he pulled the nipple and gave it a flick, I was sure he was doing it for his own amusement and paedophilic fantasies. I gave him a look as if to say that he ought to stop or I'd start screaming. He did.

"So, yes. Much smaller than the right one" he said while staring at it

"Great, how wonderful" I grabbed my top and placed it over me

"It is extremely small" he seemed so unsure

"I know, that's why I came" I folded my eyes
"It might be stress" he seemed unsure

My left breast is as flat as a pancake, whereas my right breast is inflamed like a balloon. I know they are meant to be different sizes, but this is catastrophic. The doctor seems to think it's a degenerate growth problem related to stress. My councillor thinks it might be a staggered growth swing, in which parts of the body envelope more quickly than others, meaning in a few weeks or so, everything will just match up. I don't have a clue what it is, perhaps it is stress, I have been getting very little sleep and I have been over-cutting recently. My legs are literally painted into a map of the London Underground. I have been padding up my bra with tissues, to make them look more evenly matched, it kind of works, but it makes my left one look more mushed then the right one. Maybe I will become a circus freak and people can pay me money to touch my pancake boob. Wouldn't that be sensational beyond comprehension. Nobody told *you* life was going to be this way. Why is it that in every episode of *Friends* you can see Jennifer Aniston's nipples, is that soundstage really that cold? Does Matthew Perry have a shrivelled little friend under his pants in the same scene? I have so many questions. It's the one where Harper watches

Friends for the whole day because she wants to feel sorry for herself and she couldn't give a damn about what anybody else says or thinks.

"Rouuooosssssss" says Rachel

"I just found a new dinosaur" says Ross

"Look Ross, it's my nipples"

"Oh, they are all pointy, like Madonna"

"It hasn't been my nipples' day, week or month or even their year" she sings, which is weird

"Seriously, have a look at this dinosaur"

"It's so big, what will we tell Monica?"

Monica enters.

"What the hell is that?" says Monica Gellar

"My new dinosaur" says a smiling Ross

"I need to cleeeeaaaannnn it now" she says

"You always clean" laughs Rachel

"I also cook sometimes and Richard"

"Richard!! Oh no! What will we tell Chandler Bing?!" Cries a sad Ross

"Seriously, my nipples!" she twiddles them

Chandler enters with Joey.

"Is that a giant meatball sub?" drools Joey

"No, it's a dinosaur" says Ross

"*How you doing?*" he winks at it

"Could I *be* any more Chandler?"

47

"Monica cleans Richard" shouts Rachel

"RACHEL!" Monica is very annoyed now

"Is this true?" says Chandler Bing

"I'm sorry" she holds him

Phoebe enters.

"Smelly cat, smelly cat...." She sings

Chapter 9.

It was the Summer of 1964 and Harper Goodview, *that's me*, was rumbling 'round her California beach-house, she was held side-ways, with her eye brimmed against the opening of a mighty pickle jar, the brine had gone bad, and the stickiness of the now dry, pasty and foul smelling juice, held the one and single pickle into place. It was a Mexican stand-off between Harper, *which was and still is me*, and the ferocious pile of pickles. *I thought you said it was only one single pickle.* It was, the singly-est pickle around. Her hand jammed against the back of it, one solid and sweet motion-full thump would do the trick, *I thought to myself*, that's all it needed. I counted my fingers for good luck, and whack-daddy it was time to spring into warrior mode. The thump in question was fulsome and the imprint of the ridged rim of the jar glued to my hand. The pickle rumbled. But it did not fall. That rebarbative soul, it had quite a rambunctious spirit for a lonely and rotting pickle. The turgid bumps on the ass of the jar started to jeer at my playful and daring face. It meant war, and dare I say, if it is war you want, it will be war you get. *Or something clever like that.* I itched away at the peeling paper of the Sixteen-Thousand-year-old label. I folded my hand back and whizzed it right through the air, for another glorious smack-mummy smash. The pickle tap-danced, little pickle feet, back and forth, swaying and rocking. But it did not fall. What a corpulent little bitch this pickle was being right now. If I could climb into that jar and slap it in the pickle face, by lord I would do it. Oh, this ethereal injustice. I swung my eyes 'round the room of my Cali-beach-place, to try and find some sort of simple solution. I clanked the cutlery drawer open and wielded the sharpest and most nefarious knife I could. *Breath Harper remember what you are fighting for.* I stuck the knife into the gap, it was a surgical peruse. Steady cowboy, almost done it. The pickle smiled at me as I swiped at it, slow movements, easy movements. The pickle jiggled. The pickle fell out of the jar and smeared across the floor. I bent over and found the boy in my hands. A green and dry pickle. He was stretched maybe four inches wide and had this purple mark on his forehead. The faucet exploded as I twisted the knob. I washed the pickle in the hot water for a few moments and took him over to his place of sacrifice. The chopping board. I swung the knife at him, slice. His neck slivered and his body kicked. I got him down to three slices, and I chucked the remainder into the rubbish. And there I placed him, now in three circular disks, onto my freshly made, homemade, beach-house made, burger. I took a bite and I whisked it 'round my mouth, and I spat it back onto the countertop. The pickle was extraordinarily gone off, it was vile. I had to literally dump the whole burger, I tried taking the pickles off and seeing if that made it better, but the remanence of the pickle flavour remained, all my hard work, all for nothing. I flung the phone into my hands and dialled for pizza. *Did they do take-away pizza in the 60's?* But as I fastened the telephone to my ear, I heard a voice coming through from the other side.

"Harper Goodview, I have heard a lot about you" said the voice beyond my telephone

"Telephone voice, I have heard pretty much nothing about you, considering I have no idea who you are, how rude of me actually, what is your name?"

"That doesn't matter" said the voice

"Then tell me, what *does* matter?"

"I have your friend, and if you want them back in two pieces, you better come to Apple's and Third (which was probably a place in California) at 6.pm tonight, come alone"

"Why would I want them in two pieces?"

"Did I say two pieces, my bad, I meant one piece, now I sound like a tit, damn you Reginald, you always do this" said Reginald, the voice beyond my telephone

"Reginald, eh, nice name" I jeered at him

"Don't be late, or you won't enjoy what you see" laughed Reginald

"With me, there's always a good view"

I hung up the phone and clocked the time. 5.22pm. The situation had magnified now, no more was it a pickle war, now it was personal. They had Flow, and my only chance of getting her back was ordering a taxi and making my way to the address he gave me, it was easy. And, I checked, and I was about five minutes away from the place, so I made some eggs and I even had enough time for a shower.

The taxi driver was genuinely maybe the loveliest bloke I had ever met, his name was Sunshine, and he was smitten. He told me all about himself and his wife, they were trying for a baby, but he was shooting blanks. All his wife wanted was a little bashful baby and he couldn't even give her that, he felt like such a crooked and wasted man. It's always the best people that have the hardest luck. I couldn't converse with him longer unfortunately, I had to save my friend from the evil Reginald. The place was vast, a sort of mock-up version of the runway in which Will Smith and Martin Lawrence furiously have that car chase at the end of *Bad Boys*, sort of like that. There she was, dangling from a rope, by a tree, hanging over a vat of acid. Reginald stood there, he looked normal, wasn't anything too crazy off about him, seemed like anyone else really. I reached into my holster, but I had forgotten my gun. *Stupid mistake Harper*. Reginald laughed at me.

"Isn't such a good view now Sunshine"
He was talking to Sunshine, the cab driver. He had his wife, hanging over a separate vat of acid. This was way more dangerous than the pickle thing, I was way over my head. Thankfully Sunshine was a beautiful ray of, well, of sunshine. He kicked Reginald in the nuts and called it Tuesday. He saved his wife and I made my way over to Flow; I grabbed that same old knife and I went to cut the rope, but before I could, she looked at me and she started crying.

"I don't love you, why do you keep doing this?"
"What do you mean?" I say
"I don't like you, you have to accept that"
"But..."
"I always fall, you know that"

"I thought I could have saved you this time"

"It's impossible"

"Flow, I don't know what to do"

"Just leave me alone forever"

The rope snaps and Flow falls into the vat of acid. She was right, that was her biggest problem, she was always right. She would always fall, no matter how many times I replayed it in my head, no matter how many fantasies I created.

Chapter 10.

'*Don't look down*' was printed in bold purple font, on a yellow backdrop. Underneath it in small writing it read '*unbelievable prices now at Carmen's Carpets. Price drops worth falling for*'. I stopped going to the billboard every Sunday with Flow, I just found it way too soul sucking, instead we took it in turns. Every second Sunday. We would duck-tape the Virgin Mary lunchbox to the metal flooring and I would pay my bounty every week into the box and smoke at my leisure. She would take the money, pay her cousin and refill the box. It was seamless. We were theoretically falling, but we still had that little bit of a balance.

I sat under the 'd' of down and I ripped the duck-tape up off the box and tussled a beauty into my fingertips, lit her a flame and hung my head back towards the pretty, sun dipped sky. It wasn't the same without her beside me, but it was something. And, right now, I really needed something. I looked up at the word down, and then I glared down, at the down below, and I noticed how small the flowers were, and how if I jumped I would splash all the white daisies and turn them red, and how Flow would find my dead body next Sunday. She would have to tell my parents how I was this pile of mush, and she would have to live with it forever. But I didn't jump, obviously. I didn't like these new tendencies of mine, of wanting to really mess with the world, so I decided from now on it was best to not come up to the billboard alone, just in case my mind or the weed got the better of me. So, I asked Goose if he would sit with me every second Sunday, for a few hours and smoke some weed. And, he said yes. I understand how it sounds, but I didn't make friends easy, and everyone thought I was some sort of creep, he was all I had, and after leaving him that night in his car, I thought he deserved a second chance. At first it was weird, and a little uncomfortable, but soon it just became this thing, I even started to like it. He was actually quite nice, I always thought he was this big idiot, but he was deeper than that, and even though we were using each other, I kind of thought that maybe he liked being up there with me, or at least he was a really good pretender.

"If you could be anything in the world what would you be?" I turned and looked at him, with glaring wide eyes and a huge smile

"Superman" he seemed so certain

"Superman, why?"

"'Cus it's superman"

"You're an idiot" I laughed, tugging away at the joint in my mouth

"Shut up, what about you?"

"A particle. A simple and tiny particle of something much greater, something that could just get lost and exist in something more complex, and grander than whatever it happened to solely be, something worth not noticing" I said slowly

"Can I ask you a question Harper?"

"Yeah"

"Why do you even come up here?"

"What?"

"Why are we here?"

"I have been coming up here ever since..."

I froze a moment, and really thought about his question. I didn't want to think of her.

"I don't know, okay, I just do"

"Okay" he looked defeated

I bent over to grab another joint, but he stopped me, and he burnt into my eyes and he started kissing me. I didn't know what came over me, but in that moment, all I wanted was him. I tore off my clothes and he took me in his arms, and we made love under the stars. I felt safe in his arms, he held me like I was important, like

I meant something, he was the grand thing, and I was just the particle, existing inside of him. It wasn't my dead body smudged across the daisies anymore, now it was Flow's body, and I was the one to find it, and it was this constant replaying memory. She kept dying in my mind, she was dripping away from me, I tried to catch onto her, pull her up by the hair, but I couldn't hold on, she would always slip through. But I found a way to deal with it, I just stopped looking down. She was still there, I was still madly in love with her, but now I had Goose, and he kept my head above ground, and he distracted me from myself, and more importantly, he kept me from looking down.

Chapter 11.

Pulled ties and sleeves with holes in 'em, all hanging too low and white shirts with make-up 'round the collar. There was this circle of people, they were chanting and lifting their elbows. There was this sliver in the circle, a poke through of light that I could face into. Inside were two girls, fighting. Pulling at one another's hairs, spitting blood and punching teeth out. She looked different with her hair dragged through the mud. I didn't let her see me, I just grabbed hold of Goose's hand and walked away from whatever hole she was diving into, she wasn't mine to save anymore. We just drifted apart, like two halves of a turtle's shell, after a turtle dies. And the shell gets knocked around, underneath the dark of the ocean floor, until it breaks. She started hanging around with these people that called themselves *Hail*. She too had a blade, but it was made of a different kind of torture. She wasn't a bad person, none of them were, they just wanted the world to love them again, but they just kept losing.

Hail was located at this abandoned church, just beyond the new church. It was about a 15 minute walk past the billboard, which happened to have a picture of a gleaming pair of teeth, all white with the caption '*Keep Smiling*' on it, but nobody even looked up at that old thing, so nobody took any real notice.

Flow was tapping her fingers on the wooden pew; all the pews were painted in different colours, and there was graffiti everywhere. She had this dark purple eye shadow on and had these beautiful purple boots. Diamond was laid out on the floor of the alter, poking hairs out of their arms. They were looking up at the scrapes and cracks of the old church roof. They had this silk black dress on, and badly applied but artful fingernail polish. Flow was a bit broken for ware, her face was slightly bruised, and her knuckles were all scarred and burst up. Her lip was squeezed slightly on the left side, from an obvious punch to the face. She had this glint in her eye, it was blinding. She was staring at the glow of the sun refracting off the stained-glass windows. It lit her up in rainbows.

"The sun's nearly down" she said, looking through the rainbow

"You should just let it go" said Diamond

"We live by the image people sharpen us with" she bit down on her teeth

"You're just going to make things worse"

"I don't care"

60

She looked fierce, but she was lying, she did care. Do you know the exhaustion of lying to yourself, the pain of telling yourself that you're *this* person, this hole of a person that you are not? It's exhausting. The girl that she was fighting, her name was Yuki Q. She was Spongey's sponge, she was this deranged waterlily, misunderstood and imperfect. Spongey was this hell raising carrot top that sold acid to ex-con's and paralyzed veterans. He'd too often lick his own batch and serenade in his own psychedelic nightmares. Yuki Q's face always looked half broken, she had these fake teeth, from all the punching that he'd do to her. He pulled out her hoop earring one time and she had to be rushed to the hospital; she told the doctors that she caught it in a tree branch. Spongey hung out with these halfwits, with grey trackies and spikey hair, and when they talked, they never pronounced the first and last parts of words.

"I 'ellin ya, 'er's a 'ovely 'air of 'reasts 'li"
They weren't slow by any means; they were just popped out fast and made grow up almost instantly by a pack of burning cigarettes.

There's this thing called the Night of a Million Lights, it's this symbolic ceremony, celebrating the power of electricity, it happens every year, and there's always this huge party. Flow and Harper would always go to the billboard and watch as the lights flickered on and off. But this time, Flow went to a house-party, full of that brimming, let's get wicked, kind of energy. She hated parties, but she needed to show face, so she did. Spongey glared at her with his giant bug head and roach eyes. He led her to this box room with a single bed and a few children's toys on the floor. She didn't even think. The echoing sounds of torture are unrecognisable, because pain is too often muted. She didn't even shriek. She didn't even move. He forced his face on hers and kissed her. She froze a moment before she spoke up.

"I don't want to…"

"Come on" he smiled at her

"I'm sorry" she had nothing to be sorry about
He forced his fingers 'round her neck and started squeezing. Feeling every inch of her.

"I heard you are freaky" he whispered
As he pinned her down on the bed, he slid his pants down, and gleamed into her brown eyes. The dripping black ink stretched out from under her iris. He got his fingers inside her pants and pulled them down. She didn't cry, or yell, or say a single word. She just laid there and stared at the ceiling, as if nothing was

happening. The ink slowly moved down her body and bled onto the ugly blue carpet underneath. Yuki Q pounced in and went crazy. Spongey stood up, his dick sharpened by the spill of light from the hallway. He pointed at Flow and said that she was a dirty black whore, he started to cry, he was that despicable. Flow left the party and as she was walking the lonely streets, the lights all flickered out and she counted down from ten, as her and Harper would always do, every year.

"10…"

"9…"

"8…"

Nothing said *"Hold my fist, you corrosive bubbling prick"* quite like the face spread 'cross Flow's. The scabbed bloody knots added to the fervour. Diamond was blowing a chewing gum bubble out of their teeth, which seemed the most appropriate thing to do at that very moment. They were sat in the driver's seat, while Flow sat beside them. They were parked across the street from Yuki Q's house. It was only a week ago, at this very house, and Flow tried extraordinarily to wave that from her mind. It was in Yuki Q's brother's room where it happened. It just sat in the dark sky, with the blinds open, the lights were on and a little boy ran around playing with his toys, the room looked innocent.

"You okay?" Diamond popped the bubble

"It's not fair, I never asked to grow up. Everyone thinks it's so wonderful, being a child, but it's not, 'cus every day you have a new thing to deal with. And at the same time, you're growing up, and everyone around you keeps on knocking you down, they knock you down, when all you are trying to do, is grow up. Because maybe when you're older, people will be less mean, and less cruel, but it's not true. It's the same, it's worse. 'Cus now everyone knows better, but they keep on doing it. And I got blood stains that I don't think I can ever wash out, and the only solace I got, are these marketing pioneers, these well toothed assholes who say 'You ain't alone', I would rather be alone, that gives me more hope, because if we are all screwed, then what the hell is the point. Why do we stand to be fucked with, what kind of world is that?"

"I dunno" they really did not know

A car pulled up outside Yuki Q's house. It was Spongey and Yuki Q. They were arguing quite loud. Throwing words through the air at one another. After about four gloriously full minutes of constant noise they stopped. He kissed her on the lips and got into his car and drove off. Diamond took a breath and looked at Flow, who nodded her head. Diamond started the car and slowly moved behind Spongey. The streets were practically empty, and the radio played low humming in the background. Eventually Spongey stopped outside another, more sodden looking house, maybe fifteen minutes away from Yuki Q's. He waited in the car, and then the door of the house flung open. A girl walked out; it was difficult to make out anything about her. She got into the passenger's seat. Diamond looked at Flow again, as if to say, *'This seems wrong, can we just go home'*, but Spongey started his car, and Diamond followed. It was now much darker, and the headlights could only shine so far. Diamond squinted their eyes and kept behind, but not too far away as to lose him. Spongey pulled into a carpark, and he parked up. Diamond drove in and stopped. It was too far away to see anything.

"What now?" said Diamond

"The bag"

A brown paper bag sat in the backseat; it had been there the whole time. Diamond unwillingly leant back and grabbed it, handing it to Flow. She pulled her hood up and creaked the car door open. The night was cold, and she led her feet slowly towards Spongey's car. Suddenly, pouring out of her eyes, a thundering rain of ink splashed forth, the jolt whacked Flow down to her knees. Her eyes stung and the ink blasted out. After ten seconds it stopped. Diamond ran to her side and held their hand on her shoulder. The ink bubbled on the ground in front of them.

"What the fuck is going on?" they said
The ink arose from the ground and started joining. It formed a beastly monster with two beaming white eyes.

"Flow, I think we should go"
Diamond took Flow and they ran towards their car. The ink monster smudged towards Spongey, who was now outside yelling up at the beast.

"What kind of fucking magic is this?" he yelled
The ink monster stretched out their arms and impaled Spongey in the chest. The ink spread 'cross his entire body and instantaneously he imploded. His thick plum blood sprayed onto the windshield of his car. The girl sitting inside his car screamed and climbed out of the car and crept along the ground. The monster glared at the girl, and in an instant it vanished.

"We have to go" whispered Diamond
"What about the girl?"
Diamond shoved Flow into the car and quickly they drove out and away from the carpark. The girl got to

her feet and stood in the puddles of Spongey's blood. She started blubbering and screaming.

Flow and Diamond sat in the low light, a few blocks up from the happening. She froze down on her feet and wagged them back and forth.

"What was that?" she said

"I dunno"

"That girl. She looked so young"

"What's in the paper bag?"

Flow pulled the paper bag up and pulled out a hammer.

"I just wanted to scare him"

"Your eyes, are they okay?"

"Yeah. They are fine"

Diamond placed their hand on her shoulder. And grasped Flow deep in their hands. Flow held no real emotion on her face, she was still frozen solid from what had happened.

The young girl, covered in blood, tapered down the midnight streets. Her eyes were open wide, and her feet marked the ground with every step. She found herself at the front door of the police office. She waltzed in, footprints of blood. They all froze and looked at her.

"I would like to report a murder"

The police ran to her as her feet crippled to the floor. They took her inside a little room and gave her some apple juice.

"So, let me get this straight, you're saying a monster made of ink..." the policewoman stumbled

"Yes" the young girl replied

The policewoman sat beside a frightened and weak young girl. She placed her hand on her shoulder.

"My name is Jane. Here, drink some juice"

The young girl drank some more juice.

"I'm not crazy" the young girl said

"I know. Now tell me, what's your name?"

"Abi"

"And this boy?"

"They called him Spongey"

"And he was your boyfriend?"

"No. He was older. He..." she froze

"It's okay. Everything is gonna be alright"

Jane held Abi as she cried.

Flow sat smoking by a tree, outside the hail church. She still seemed ghostly. Diamond walked over and plopped a peach flavoured juice box by her feet.

"Maybe you should go talk to her"

"I let her go"

"It's never over"

Flow looked down at the juice-box and then back up at Diamond, who was smiling at her.

"You know she knew I hated these. She drank one at my dad's funeral. That's what I love about her, she doesn't listen. I was supposed be the one that kept her strong, but I am so weak. I don't know what to do anymore"

"You got trampled on"

"So did everyone else"

"Yeah, but so did you"

"What do I do now?"

"You get back up, and you keep on growing"

Diamond smiled at her, they had hope.

Chapter 12.

Diamond tore open the front door of their house. Their dad sat watching football on a small blue television set. Spooning peas out of a can, into his wide mouth.

"Where the fuck were you?" he spat

"Out" they spat back

Diamond walked through into the kitchen and ripped the fridge open, they pulled out a ready meal. Grabbed a fork from the drawer and poked little holes into the plastic sheet. They slumped the meal into the microwave and pressed it on for two minutes.

"You look like a fucking princess" their dad knocked into the kitchen and pulled a beer out from the fridge

"Diana, or you thinking more like Cinderella?"

"Watch your fucking tongue boy"

"I ain't no boy"

"You are one queer fuck"

Diamond tightened their fist and took a big breath and watched as their dad left the kitchen. They unclenched their fist and the microwave dinged. They took their ready meal and pulled the plastic sheet off the top. The steam poured out. They sat at the kitchen table. The noise of the television echoed through the house.

After they finished, they went upstairs. Their room was plain and small. They had a little card on their desk, from their grandmother. It read: My little boy, I hope you grow up to be a beautiful young man. They kept it there because it was important to them, their grandmother died before they came out, before they really discovered who they were.

"I grew up gram" and they kissed the card They slipped out of the dress and kicked off their shoes, it had been a mad fucking night. They cradled into their sheets and shut their eyes.

Flow stood by the cemetery gates with Diamond. They watched from afar as the coffin dropped into the ground. They still didn't understand how this had all happened. Flow hated him, and yet, she never got any chance to let him know, how much he really messed her up, how much it hurt, how much he ruined her. She nodded her head, and they both walked away. Diamond gave her a little smile, and she smiled back. The air was fresh, the garbage had been taken out and the sun was shining in the sky. Flow looked up at the billboard. It read '*Hello, again*' with a slogan underneath '*it's never too late to reconnect*'.

Chapter 13.

"Hello, again" said Flow

"I thought you hated juice-boxes?"

"It's for you" she unfurled her hand

"Thanks"

I poked the straw's hard edge out from under the plastic covering. It was a peach flavoured juice. I stabbed the straw into the foil hole and slurped some juice into my mouth. Flow took a seat beside me, the metal bars squished against her. She waved her boots in the high airs, as she always used to do. It was this strange memory that was happening in real time. Her smile had slid away down a drain someplace, I could tell she had this unspoken fissure inside of her lips. She looked different, almost crushed open.

"How's Goose?" she said

"Really good"

"Have you...?"

"Yeah..."

"I'm happy for you" she tried to smile

The space in her lips expanded and closed, and it kept happening. I want to ask why she bleeds, why she breaths into plastic and why she looks so broken, but I

72

can't. I reached out my hand, and I placed it on her shoulder, and I could feel the heat of her skin; she was wearing a string top.

"I am so sick of running" she said

"Then don't"

She turned her head, and the crease in her neck folded inwards, and her lips looked dry and tarnished and her eyes bloody and red. She ran her teeth slowly down her lower lip, as she stared into my eyes. I swear she was about to cry.

"I am sorry…"

She lifted her head into mine and started kissing me, her breath filled my lungs. I could feel every morsel of her body, all the broken arteries. She grabbed my breasts and I ran my hands down the sides of her. She pulled up my top and I tried to do the same to her, and undo her bra, but couldn't quite get it undone. She took her hands behind her back and undid it, smiling at me while she did. She smudged her palms on my bare breasts and I closed my eyes and saw nothing but light. She began moving downwards, but I stopped her, and I opened my eyes and I could see the dreary sky.

"What are we doing?" I pushed her away

She looked at me, her eyes on mine.

"Harper…"

I turned my body into itself. The air filled with a thick silent screaming. Flow locked her fingers into mine and I was in her hands again.

"Something happened me Harper"

"You can tell me anything"

"That night, when you kissed me, something happened to me"

"What happened?"

"I found myself"

Love is such a boring word to describe something so spectacular, and so defining. In that moment, I understood it. Flow was my blade, she was my torture, that one thing that took over, that bled and cut through me. But she was also the warm water and the band-aid, she was what killed me, but every time she would bring me right back to life.

Chapter 14.

Place is a mess down here; we lost a lot of good hemp. I am Rodney, eh, I am just a simple old joint really. It's been some time, yanno. I just gotta keep myself busy, keep doing things, no matter what they are. I wanna be smoked, I wanna be cuddled up in her fingers, feel the pressure of 'em against my body. It's what we all want. I was in this haze, I believed in the power of the dent, but I don't think I do anymore. Sometimes I just sit and look at it, and hope that the power somehow drains me, but it never does. I started this weekly thing, this sort of club, a place for us to talk about our problems.

"It's a constant thing, knowing I am a drug" says Bibby one of the cleverer joints

"I hear ya" everyone mutters

"People think I am bad, but I don't think I am bad, I am just me" she says

"Say it again" everyone chants

"I never asked to be rolled, I just was"

"Thank you, Bibby," I say

The joints that come to the meetings, they just wanna feel more alive. There's this wave of arrogance and hatred on the outside. The world beyond the box. They wanna smite us, they wanna tear our papers up and throw our 'bac in the toilet bowl. It's painful, being told you were built for all the wrong reasons. It's just, we see it differently, we see a world of shiny metallic walls, inside this lunchbox. I keep staring at my own reflection, I wanna try understand me, the humanity of a joint. I want to bash my head against the wall, just to get a chance to poke at my brain and see what makes it tick. Bibby is right, I wasn't asked to be rolled. There's always someone who wants to kill you, and it always feels like there's no one that wants to love you, even though that's not true, there's always someone, but it's hard to let yourself live by that standard. All we got down here are the metal walls.

"You looking at yourself again?" says Bibby

"Can't help it, it's all reflecting on me"

"Yeah, that's the trouble"

"I poked out the lid earlier"

"Lucky"

"They are together again"

"Are you sure?"

"It's what I saw"

"Good for them"

"They looked happy"

"It's one thing to look it"

Rod melts his eyes into the metal walls.

"What's wrong Rod?"

"Maybe they are right"

"Who?"

"The ones that say we are bad"

"They just don't like what's different"

"You always have a bright outlook on things"

"I want to see the outside do better, that's all"

"Where would you like to light?"

"On a boat, in the middle of the sea, with the moon in the sky, and the waves hitting against the sides, splashing my papers a little"

"That would be nice"

"Yeah, and you?"

"I hear being passed 'round is pretty nice"

"I guess once the lighter is good, does it even matter where we ember?"

"Guess not"

"You don't got to keep looking at the walls for something Rod. What if what you're searching for is already right inside of you"

"I just feel like I need something more"

"You don't find the gold without a map"

"Problem is, I don't want the gold"

"You want what's not on the map"

"Yeah"

"Rod?"

"Uh huh"

Bibby grabbed me and kissed me. She pulled me down and beyond the embossed dotted curve in the box, behind the second partition. Her papers were soft, and her packing was stuffed all the way full. She started to twist my top, and I let her for a moment until I pulled back.

"What are you doing?"

"Trust me"

"Okay" I always did trust her

She twisted and twisted until I had a perfect twist. She looked at me, and she smiled. Suddenly the box started shaking and the top opened. Flow's big eyes gleamed down into the lunchbox.

"Eh. This one is already twisted"

Flow poked her hand in and caught me into her fingers, she pressed on my sides with force and I could feel the blood rush to my head. I was flying through the sky, and the birds were so beautiful. She slowly closed the box, and Bibby shouted up.

"No more metal walls"

The lid closed over. Flow was sitting behind a closed

down comic store. She was with Harper, and two other people, I didn't know who they were. I heard the lighter fluid spark and my head exploded. I was passed 'round between the four of them. I could see them all smile, and laugh and I knew then, in that very moment, my very last moment, that I wasn't bad, and they were wrong.

Chapter 15.

The shining perplex glass reflected the four of us so smoothly. Flow was holding the joint in her hands, she took a drag and passed it along. The sun was beating down and my eyes were watering from squinting too heavy. I guzzled my nose against the glass and smeared my hands over my eyes and peered in at the colourful abyss of comic covers and plastic toy figures. I slumped back down against the side of the building and crossed my legs over Flow. Goose and Diamond were there too. I had told Goose all about everything, and I thought he'd flip out and go nuts, but he never did. He said he was happy for me, and that he always had this inkling, but never said anything 'cus he was too afraid of losing me. He might have looked like a dick, but he was sweet, and even with everything that had happened, he was one of my closest friends, and I was happy that he stayed around, I still needed him. In a weird way, him and Flow were similar, it was as if they were carved from the same tired piece of rock. Flow introduced me to Diamond a few weeks back, and I was immediately wanting to be around them more and more. Yanno when someone has that special aura, that lucid, acid-like, healing kind of energy, that was illuminating all out of Diamond, and I wanted more of it. The joint came into my fingers and I took a big breather of it, the smoke railed its way down my lungs, and I could feel the kick of flames start to take me away. I exhaled. I passed it on. I wasn't used to being grounded during my highs, I was so used to sitting up on that billboard, that this new down on earth high felt strange, unexplainable. The metal of the billboard was undergoing a lick of paint. It was this scheme set up by the local council called 'Colour of Tomorrow'. It was a way of getting people out of the house, and joining arms as a community to paint different buildings and local landmarks, the billboard was due a lick of paint and so we were crumbled up by the closed down comic store, in a dirty alleyway by the bins. Heaven. But it was nice, being together. I had never really had a group of friends before.

Flow turned away the joint and stood up, and I knew trouble was lurking inside of her mind. I squelched my eyelids close and prayed she wasn't going to do something stupid. But the girl is fire, she grabbed a half beaten down brick from behind the bins and yelped it against the glass and shattered it whole. We all bounced up, covered in shards of glass. She looked ahead, at all the colour.

"After you, Madame" she grinned out loud
I shook my head and walked over the glass and through into the comic store. The place smelled, and the carpets were all nibbled and full of dust. I walked further in and I could see this strange figure, I jumped out of my skin in fright. But it was only this cardboard cut-out of some superhero.

"Look at this" Flow called out
I walked over and she was flicking through a comic, she pointed at a backdoor that said, *'Do not enter'* and she smiled and threw the comic on the floor. Don't ever tell Flow what not to do, because she will always do it. She creaked the handle a few times, but the door wouldn't budge.

"It's jammed shut"
She tried kicking it down, but still it wouldn't budge. She looked around the room, hoping to find some sort of magic way in, she stared me down, and plucked a clip out from my hair. She twisted it open and began to unlock the door. She fiddled that clip around for five minutes straight, we all just watched her do it. Voila. It opened, she looked back at me and smirked. I laughed at her and we poked our way into this forbidden chasm. It was dark and foreboding, full of

cobwebs. Diamond flicked on and off the light switch, but the power wasn't working. Goose pulled his phone out and shone the torch around the room, it was plain and uninteresting, as you would expect from a comic bookstore back room. That was until we found all these strange carvings on the desk, scribbles and cuts, and marks, some done in pen and others in blade. They all said the exact same thing. *'Beware'*

"Fuck" whispered Flow from across the room I looked over, and when I saw what she had seen, I nearly melted. It was a body of a girl, hanging from her belt. Her eye sockets were wide, and her eyes were missing. They were two big black voids. A puddle of black tar bubbled under her dangling feet. It fizzed and popped. The edge of a book hung out of the tar. I dipped my hand in and wiped it clear. It was her diary. We all looked at each other, I opened the diary and started to read.

Chapter 16.

The diary of Lucy Grotowski.

10/04/04 7.22pm

Today was a crazy day. I woke up as normal, my hair was tawny, and my eyes were almost glued shut from all the crust between the folds. I went for a quick shower, to try and wake myself up. I remember looking into the mirror. I was standing naked, with my nipples hard and my skin dripping wet. I had a prickly brush of hair down below, I flicked it 'round my fingers, all the follicles and strands. I dried myself off, and I got on with my morning routine. I do this strange thing every morning, I toast 2 slices of bread, and then I put the toast into a sandwich maker, but I don't put any fillings in, just butter, and lots and lots of it too. I leave it a few moments and then I have this buttery explosion of toast. I do an egg or two sometimes, but today I didn't really feel like it. I wore this itchy uniform to school, with a bold crown as the crest, yellow and blue. I wore tights and a skirt; it had these tapered folds. After the end bell, Imelda, Tess, J and I went to Rushmore Park, we drank some four loco we robbed from a 7-11; the Indian man running the tills was arguing with an elderly lady about cigarettes. It was supposed to be peach flavoured but tasted more like apple. We watched some of the Mexican boys play soccer in the field. Tess told us that Rainn was having this big party tonight, and that we should all go. Rainn was this brown skinned nightmare; he would get himself into all sorts of terror. One time in Lake Mohoe, he was naked pissing into the water and the police caught him and he had to sleep in a cell, and they called his parents. He got grounded for three weeks. He was rich, his father had invented some sort of metal that was used in car manufacturing. Tess and Rainn are dating, but she expects all of us to somehow be involved in it, it's annoying. I said I'd go. I still need to pick out something to wear. Tess and J went off to buy drugs and Imelda and I kept drinking. She told me about her father's new lover, and how they have obnoxiously loud sex. I listened. After a while a few of the Mexicans walked over to us and we all chatted about school and the way the weather was so warm and nice. Julio sat close beside me, he had this big chest and hair on his back. His friends grew tired after an hour and they all waved goodbye, but Julio stayed. He was red faced and had a big plump nose. He told us all about his future, how he wanted to be a soccer player, we just nodded along to what he was saying. Every minute he stayed in that sun, sitting beside us, the more handsome he was becoming. I don't know what came over us really, maybe it was the beer, maybe it was his chest, maybe it was the sun. We walked with him to his car. Imelda sat in the backseat and I was up front with him. He drove us to his house. His parents were at work. His room was messy, and his bed was all squeaky. Imelda took her top off first, and her breasts were big and round. I took my top off after she did, my breasts were more triangular shaped, but they were still big. We started kissing, she had soft lips. Julio watched as we kissed, he looked happy. We both got on our knees and unbuttoned his pants and took it out. It was big and scary looking. I had him in my mouth while Imelda pulled her hands through my hair. After a few minutes he told us to get onto the bed, and we did. He got inside of Imelda. He went at her hard. He moved to me next, and then back to Imelda, all in different positions. He finished on both of our faces and we wiped it off with our shirts. He dropped us back to the park and we didn't really talk about it. She said she will be going to the party tonight; I hope it won't be too weird.

11/04/04 3.43am

I am so drunk right now.

11/04/04 1.47pm

I just drank a pint of Orange Juice; it had no pulp. I washed it 'round my teeth, trying to eliminate the taste of rusting vodka and shitty Red Bull mixer. My lips are all chapped, I must have been kissing someone, I can't fully remember. I didn't see Imelda at the party, but I have a message from her saying she was feeling a bit sick. I am pretty sure it's an excuse, she's obviously awkward about everything that happened with Julio. I don't blame her. Rainn let off fireworks last night, all the colours, it was beautiful. I stood in the middle of the dirt of the party, letting the shining blasts of colour blur me over. I could see rainbowed reflections savagely sucking the life out of my eyes. But I liked it. I kept looking up. I can't remember much else, only those shocking bursts of colour.

16/04/04 11.22pm

Don't fuck with me, if you can't cope with me. I told him not to go there, I told him not to push me. He does this, he never stops doing stupid shit. All the time. He has this temper, he just lashes out and goes crazy, like bat-shit motherfucking crazy. I wanted to protect my friend; she was just standing there watching him explode. Tess is like that; she lets shitty things happen all around her and she just stands and watches it melt. So, I stepped in and told him to calm down, that Tess was only saying, and she was right, that it's a bad idea to keep pushing it. He wanted Mercutio, this black kid from East Chester, to admit that he had this thing for Tess. And that he'd quote on quote 'batter that butternut scotch head off him'. He went at me, being all like, none of your business Lisa, get down from that stupid stool of yours, get outta my shit. I told him to fuck it. He took his fist at me, not making contact, but he had this aggression. I pushed him and he rattled me with his fist, into my side. I whacked against the pavement and Tess just stood there. I grabbed a sharp stone from the ground and stabbed it into his foot. It seared right down into the skin, and blood started dribbling out from under his shoe. I spat into the wound, to add extra taste. I got up and limped away, as Tess ran to his side. You really ought to know who your friends are. I have this picture frame on my wall, it's Jesus with a crown of thorns, and he is bleeding from his skull. But he does not scream, and he does not cry. The word hail is printed on it, and I keep looking at it. I can't stop looking at it.

20/06/04 3.43pm

I saw Rainn today; his cheekbones were all bruised and poking out. They looked all yellow and gooey, as if a bee had made sex to them. We went behind the back of the old bowling alley building and he took me up against the bins and did me good. We did it bare and without much love. It's strange, you stab a guy in the toe, and he pushes you to the floor, and somehow, all you wanna do is fuck the living dick off him.

31/11/04 (no time written down)

If Tess says another damn word, I will chew her face off. She keeps going on about this wildflower, has an eating disorder. I don't think she sees me writing this, she is so soberly fascinated with her own mouth. Egotistical tramp.

02/12/04 5.44pm

It snowed today. It's beautiful in a way, all the squishy white snow covering the roads. The roofs of cars look like the insides of pillows. Jesus keeps looking at me, as if he knows it's his birthday month. I just smile at him and keep writing. There was a big write up in the papers today about this billboard being erected beside the church, and everyone is going crazy.

03/12/04 3.35pm
Rainn is dead.

?????? (no date or time recorded)
May this be my last recorded note. I did not kill Rainn. I was having a sexual affair with him, but I did not kill him. I don't know how he died. Before he died, he text me something peculiar, it simply read. 'I am sorry for living'. I assume he offed himself, but the doctors say he was murdered. There is a strangeness in this town. Beware.

I sat next to Flow on the freshly painted billboard, breathing in the new paint fumes. She dangled her bare feet over the edge. I looked out at the world. Flow stopped moving her feet and she looked at me, I didn't look at her, but I could feel her looking at me. I could feel all her weight.

"Harper, I must tell you something"
I didn't respond, I just sat glaring out.

"There was this guy…"
As she spoke, I watched the movements of people, all shuffling out of the church. Not knowing what Flow

was saying to me, not knowing how much it hurt me, to hear every single word she said.

"...he uh...he took me into a room..."

Soon the people had all left. Time was passing but suddenly Flow stopped talking, as if she couldn't finish her story. I watched a small bird pick rubbish off the ground. I couldn't look at her, I didn't know how. I reached my hand out and grabbed hers. I pointed at the small bird.

"I think that's a robin"

Flow looked at the bird. She took my hand and we both watched as the robin poked at the ground. We must have watched that bird for a whole hour.

"Those scribbles, in that room"

"Beware" she said it so pointed

"She was just hanging there..."

"I must show you something"

We climbed down from the billboard and she took me through some fields, it was a good twenty-minute walk. And then we got there. It was beautiful. An old abandoned church, all painted in different colours. Spray-painted onto the side was the phrase *'Hold All in Love'*. Flow looked at my wonder filled face. I caught her eyes.

"It's a place for people who don't belong"

"I don't understand"

We stumbled into the church and an old picture of Jesus hung on the wall, with the word hail printed on it. A crude L and R with a love heart was carved inside. It looked like it had been there forever.

"It's a place for dying flowers to heal"

"The girl from the store, she went here?"

"I am not sure"

"Flow?"

"Yeah"

"I am sorry I left you"

"That's okay. I left you too"

Flow looked at me, and I looked at her. It had been such a long day; it had been such a long life.

Chapter 17.

Mum stood by the front porch smoking, as dad closed the car boot shut. Flow and I sat on the wall, and dad gave me the nod, it was time. I took a deep breath. Flow grabbed me 'round and kissed me on the lips, full and real. I didn't even care that my parents were watching.

"I got you something"

She pulled out this perfectly wrapped box. With a blue ribbon and beautiful gold wrapping paper. She told me not to open it until I got there. I couldn't seem to leave her eyes, she pushed me softly on the shoulder.

"Go, I'll see you in a few weeks"

My front teeth were perched on my lower lip, the warmest of airs blew through the gap. I smiled through the heat and threw my hands 'round her body. Then I pulled away and walked towards the car. My mum had quenched the cig and was now waiting for my hug, which I gave her, less intense and special than the one I gave Flow, but it was still nice. She lit another cig and I got into the front passenger seat of the car. Dad was sitting by the wheel, before he turned the key, he looked at me, he didn't really say anything, but I knew exactly what he meant. He turned the ignition and he pulled out of the driveway. Flow stood on the wall and started dancing, just as she used to do during school. I laughed and then when she left my field of view, I felt sad. I looked down at the gift in my arms. I held it tight, it was all I had left of Flow. I turned the radio loud. I let my hair down and I watched as the world I once knew passed me by.

The room was tidy, as in it was very neatly small and compact, it was simple. There was a white painted desk, which looked extremely cheap and flimsy, it rocked from side to side with a single finger push. The lamp shade was slightly torn, and the mattress was springy and loud. But the view from the window was beautiful. It was a green paradise of flowers and trees. There was a small bathroom, but nothing crazy. It was just a simple bathtub and a toilet and sink. Dad climbed up the stairs with the last box and he placed it on the mattress, next to all the others.

"That's it. The last of it"

"I guess it's real now"

"You'll love it"

"I know"

He stood and he looked at me, and then he gazed 'round the room and then he fiddled his keys and then he looked at me once more.

"I should let you settle in"

"Thanks dad, for everything"

He smiled, with a slight pain folded into the flaps. He gave me a real big hug and then he left. I sat on the spare space on the mattress, amongst the crowd of boxes. I took Flow's gift into my arms and I started ripping the golden paper off. It was her Virgin Mary lunchbox; I opened the lid and inside was a handwritten note. And there were about thirty pre-rolled joints. And a silver flip lighter. I stood up, cocked the window open and sat on the little lip, pulled a joint out and plopped it into my mouth. I took the lighter and flipped it open. I ripped the flame on the head of the joint and I inhaled. I looked out at all the beautiful flowers, I thought of Flow, and of how much I already missed her. But I also thought about this new adventure, and how for once in my life, I was doing something that I wanted to do. I finished the joint and I caught glance of all the boxes. I breathed heavily out my nostrils and I started unpacking.

The next morning, I was walking through the cobblestones of the college, the buildings were so grand, and I kept looking up at the roofs and the way they bled into the clouds of the sky. I sat underneath a big tree in the centre of the court. I was writing notes into a little pad. I had a cig in my mouth, and I puffed away at it.

"Do you have a light?" he said
I looked up from my pad and this middle eastern boy with small eyes was looking at me. Holding a cig in between his fat and ugly fingers. I handed him my silver lighter and he lit his cig up. He handed it back and sat down beside me.

"I'm Eron" he smiled
"Harper"
"The buildings are all so big"
"I keep looking up at the sky"
Eron leant his neck at the sky, and he blew his smoke upwards. He bent his head down at the ground and at his shoes, and then he looked at me.

"Thanks for the lighter"
He stood up and went to leave.

"If you wanna hang out sometime…"
He stopped and turned around.

"Yeah. That'd be nice…"
He grabbed a pen from his pocket and wrote his number on my hand. He walked away and I looked at the numbers, all random.

Chapter 18.

It was the summer before final year in high school. I remember it as if it was yesterday. We were swigging a bottle of vodka in the playground of this closed down community school. Flow was twisting the swing 'round and over itself, and then letting go, making her spin back and forwards a few times. The metal clanked and made this nasty sound. I sat on one of those twisting disk things, just sipping away from the mouth of vodka. Goose and Diamond were laid out on the safe play foam floor, looking at the starry sky. It was moonlight dark, and if we stood close, we could only see our features shining in the moon's glow. I spun the disk back and forth with my foot on the ground. The bottle of vodka had a picture of a duck. It was this pale blue colour and the vodka looked like water, the way it flowed around inside of it. I was drinking way too fast, and when it poured down my throat, it was this stinging pain, but I liked how it made me feel. Invincible and young, with my whole life down at the bottom of it. And I never slowed, I just kept knocking it back until I could feel rainbows in my eyes. There was a wire gauze fence that surrounded the school, and sometimes a few cars would pass by, and I would try and imagine who the people driving the cars looked like. I had to squint to see the cars. It made me laugh thinking of all the strange people. There was one car that I thought about a lot. It was normal, just like all the others, but I imagined a fat man with this big nose that hung like a penis down to his chest, and it really made me laugh. He would go to work with this huge penis nose drooping onto his keyboard and it would accidently press all the wrong keys. It sometimes would dip into his fresh mug of coffee and he would jump up in pain and the air dynamics would make it flop around and whack him in the chest. When he fucked it swung around like crazy, slapping against his naked fat body. Flesh on flesh sound. It really made me laugh.

"Pass the v" Flow was now standing on the swing, waving back and forth
I got up and when I did, I could feel the ground move around like waves. It rippled at my toes. I staggered my way over to the swing set and I passed Flow the vodka and sat down on the other swing, but I didn't move around, I felt too dazed. She took the bottle up high and took a swig. I told her about the fat penis nose man, and she laughed a little, but not a lot. Diamond arose and they had this baggie that they held up. Flow

drifted down from the sky and jumped off the swing and rushed towards the baggie.

"Is that crack?" she said

"Beautiful, right?" they said

She rolled some into a joint, and we smoked it. The high was glorious, but the smell was off-putting. I remember thinking, we were all riding on this big rainbow train, through the clouds. The train driver was the man with the penis nose, and he let us all touch it, and sometimes he would swing it about and make whistle noises out the nostrils. We all laughed, and we all cried, because life was living us, and we wanted so badly to live it.

I walked home with Flow after the high, and the comedown was crushing. I kept my head low and counted the steps between the white lines on the black tar of the roads. Flow would say some inaudible words now and again, but I couldn't quite understand what it was she was trying to say, and I never asked what she meant. I didn't have it in me, I just kept counting. 1...2...3...4...5 and I would walk the line, trying not to fall off, and then I would count again. I noticed that Flow was no longer beside me, and I turned around and she was standing a few steps back. She was crying. I walked over to her, and she didn't have to say anything. I swung my hands around her, and I counted. I must have counted to a thousand. I just kept counting.

"I don't...how can..."

I still couldn't understand what she was trying to say. And then she said it. And I understood.

"I must be dreaming"

When she said this, I held her extra hard. My fingers were spread wide, and I tried to hold every corner of her body. I couldn't let her go. She coughed and she cried, and I held her. I wasn't counting anymore.

Eron was sitting in the corner of my room underneath the windowsill, he looked high as hell. His eyes were melting out from under his lids. He didn't seem too interested in my story, it was as if he stopped listening somewhere in the middle, but he responded like he knew all about it.

"That's some first time"

"Yeah..."

I liked talking to him, even if he didn't really listen, it was nice to have someone. He stood up and he looked at me, it was a look of poison. I wish I knew it then, but it was the reflection in his eyes of me, that was the poison. That was always the poison. He took me in his hands, and I took him. I pulled off his clothes and he pulled off mine. He was in me, and I was yelling for more, and I watched my ceiling fan swirl. I was living my life, but I really wish it had been living me.

Chapter 19.

My feet were hanging out from the covers of my bed. *In Rainbows* was playing on vinyl. Thom Yorke's voice kept me still and comforted. I looked down at the shape of his eyes on his face. They were closed as he slept. His nostrils squashed in and out as he spoke the breath out in thunderous blasts. The condom was flopped on the brim of my metal bin, it looked like a clear banana skin hanging on the edge of a tree. I hate the morning after. The guitars in *Bodysnatchers* were loud and I was surprised that it didn't budge him. He waved his toes 'round a bit, but it was nothing more than that. I pretended to play the guitar in my head, I had this fever dream of smashing my imaginary guitar over his fat face once the song ended. But I didn't. I wanted to wake him up and tell him to get out, but I couldn't find the power. I just laid there, with his arm around me, and I pretended I was anywhere else. Absolutely anywhere else. I tilted my head to the left, and looked far beyond the condom, and the bin, and looked out at the flowers outside my window. They reminded me of Flow, and it made me feel good and bad all at the same time. The smell of latex and body sweat and the noise of drums and guitars and Thom Yorke softly screaming, and him snoring, and me thinking. It was all so much. I couldn't breathe, yet I couldn't stop.

Classes were okay. The lecture halls were way too big, and the ugly green cushions on the wooden chairs were ripped open and ragged. The desks were attached; it was as if they were teaching us to share. I was learning about Art History, and the teacher was this plump lady in her mid-fifties who always wore a turquoise cardigan and yellow shoes. Her name was Misses Lumen. She talked with a twist in her thighs, as if every word hurt her, she almost fell to the floor every time she finished her sentences. The guy next to me was doodling swastikas on his notepad, and pictures of dead horses, and premature babies crawling up trees. He was cross hatching one of the babies with his biro, he was taking his time and really putting effort into it. I watched his pen move around the page; it was numbing my brain. The date 1654 was on the whiteboard in block letters, big and bold and I had no idea why, it most probably had something to do with what was pouring out of Lumen's lips, but I wasn't listening. I kept looking at the babies crawling up the tree. There were three babies, and they looked all gooey and made of tar. I watched the hands of the clock now, and it was nearly time to leave, tick, tock, tick, tock and bang. The bell rang and I was the first up and the first out. I ran into the girl's bathrooms and my fingers kept sticking to everything I touched. I noticed this tar forming around me, in the cracks of my fingers and 'round my skull and 'round my hips. It was black and it was heavy. I was submerged in this thick black goo. In the mirror all I could see were the whites of my eyes. I was one of the tar babies. Her beautiful face was carved into the mirror in blood. She mouthed at me. She screamed.

"CHEATER!" she spat blood in my eyes

I smashed the bathroom window and crawled through the cracked glass. It sliced through my sides and blood poured out of all the newly formed holes. I was now blood and tar. I dragged across the grass and over to the tree in the middle of the court, and I started climbing. I used the tar as glue. I was a tar baby climbing up a tree. When I got to the top, the clouds were above my skull and my eyes were small, and the blood had stopped. I slipped from the branches of the tree and I hit the ground hard. The blood that smeared from my ears, took the shape of her body. Her blood-filled fingers fondled my face. She poured into me. Her plum red lips whispered.

"I thought you loved me" the blood ran out
My eyes were kaleidoscopes. And she was everywhere.
I wanted to crumble up and die.

I looked over at his brown, and fat face. I watched him snore, in and out, and I really thought about killing him. I dreamt about doing to him, what I could never do to myself. But then he opened his eyes and he looked at me. He grabbed my face and he kissed me. Thom Yorke was still screaming. And somewhere far away, in a forgotten place, is a place where the tar babies climb trees, but no matter how hard we look for it, that place is a place we will never find, and those poor tar babies will live forever knowing that they were always destined to die, alone and afraid. Forever.

Chapter 20.

When I was ten my grandfather died. I didn't know how to feel, I didn't really know the man that much. He was a drunk, he lived in this small box house. I went there once. He did all these fantastic paintings, mum used to show them to me. A lot of elephants and tigers. He was trying to find colour. I think mum blamed herself for his death, she changed when he died. Something happened to her, I can't explain it. You know when a light flickers out but it doesn't burst, it just gets warmer and more blurred, that's what happened mum. She was cold, and all my friends feared her, expect Flow. Flow and her seemed to understand each other, I think because they both lost their fathers, it made them symbiotic. Sometimes I think she preferred Flow over me. Just the way she looked at her. I told my parents I was bi when I was 12. They had these red faces on, and they didn't ask too many questions, mum looked the same way she did when she told me grandad died. It was as if I had now died too. She worked at this laundrette place at the time, she was taking night classes at the local college. She wanted to be a nurse, which I never could understand. She never cared for me, but maybe she thought by doing something good, by caring for others, that it would scrub away all the shitty things she had done. She graduated, and then she started working long hours, night-time. I saw less of her around the house, and although I sort of hated her, I missed seeing her around.

When I was young, and dad had work, she would stay in bed some mornings, she would say she was feeling sick, and I would have to walk to school. I was seven or eight and I would walk fifteen minutes to school. I took these shortcuts through dark alleyways and now that I look back on it, I realise how dangerous it was. Dad found out about it, and from the age of nine onwards, he would drive me to school. I don't know if mum was really sick. Maybe she was, but I don't know. We have never talked about it, sometimes I think it's easier to just not talk about things. I am my mother's daughter. I told her I wanted to go to art college, and I could see that she hated it. It's what her dad did, and he was dead. All the good he had ever done, was in his paintings. The elephants never did any wrong. The tigers didn't get pissed up and punch their wife in the face, they were simply just colours on canvas. And now, I wanted to do what he did. I wanted to find colour. She looked at me, and she always said things so bluntly.

"Do whatever you want"

What a cold-hearted bitch. Seriously, how hard is it to say something nice. All I wanted was some recognition, that my life wasn't just a blister on her cold and blank face. That I was a spark, or a light that she wanted. I needed her to say, 'I can see you', but she never did. But maybe I am being too mean, maybe when she said 'do whatever you want', she meant it, as in, she wanted me to be whoever I wanted to be, that her accountability for that was nulled anyways, she didn't care, because she *didn't* care. No matter what I wanted to do or be, she was happy, knowing that I was myself. Maybe.

When my grandad died, he took my mum with him. He was buried in the ground, in a casket made of wood, and the worms were eating his brain. But my mum had it worse, she was buried alive. And she never asked anyone to help her. She was cold, and mean, but she was strong, I will give her that. When Eron looked at me, in the morning, after I had fucked him, and he grabbed my face and kissed it. I didn't think about Flow, or about him, or about me. I thought about my mum. I thought about all the terrible and shitty things she had done, and I thought, that's me. I am all those things. And now, when I think of her, I don't think she's so bad anymore, because she never really was. She was just like me, in a small way, she was like everyone, she wanted what we all wanted. To walk through the fire, without getting burnt.

I pulled away from his mouth and I looked at his round eyes. They were bubble shaped and deep sunken. He had this green slice in the brown of the left one.

"My grandad died 10 years ago today"
He looked at me, much sadder now.

"Shit, I am sorry" he said
"It's okay, you didn't kill him. Did you?"
"What, no..."
"I am joking, you idiot"
"Oh, yeah. Of course. How'd he die?"
"Mum found him swinging in his closet"
"Fuck"
"Yeap"

I got out of bed and I pulled the needle off the record. My feet were bare, and the ground was cold. I cranked the window open, and the breeze hit my forehead, and it was nice. I grabbed Flow's lunchbox from the ground and clicked it open. I pulled the note out and squeezed it in my hands.

"Last night was a mistake"

"What do you mean?" he was sitting up

"I was high"

"You said you wanted it"

"I did, but I shouldn't have"

"That doesn't make any sense"

"I did it because I was sad"

"Jesus, thanks"

"It was fuck you, or cut myself"

He was silent. He didn't say anything else, he got dressed fast and he left, and when the door shut, it made a loud bang. I got one of the joints from the box and I lit it up, I was my mother's daughter. When I had the joint done, I put on a long jumper and some shoes, and went down to the nearest pharmacy. I told the nurse that I needed the morning after pill, which I didn't. I just needed someone to talk to, it's funny, the lengths you'd go to just have someone to talk to. I told the nurse all about my mum, I said that she was a nurse too, and I laughed, and I cried. When it was done, I saw that they sold electric razors, and I bought one, I thought fuck it. I got home and I beheld my sloped face in the mirror, and I did not smile. I plugged the razor in, and I shaved the hair off my head. My grandad might have been a dick, but he got one thing right, colour won't fix anything. Life's fucked, so go nuts. I looked good bald. I left the hairs on the tiles and I climbed back into bed, and I rolled my head into the pillow and closed my eyes. I was too sick to go to school. I understood my mum now.

Chapter 21.

A naked model stood in the middle of the room. She was a larger lady, with small fluffy hairs under her neck. I was studying the ripples on her belly, swinging my pencil in slow motions to create the shapes. My teacher was this slow faced man from Slovakia, he had thunder hair; it screamed at you. He always said: Don't be extraordinary, just be good enough to get yourself a haircut every week. He didn't follow his own advice. His accent was funny; it sounded like the Swedish chef.

"Don't a eva stup a lewking at the body"

The body was a golden apple. It formed who we were. All the tiny finger bones, all the way to that bit at the tip of your nose that you can circle around in your fingertips. We drew a lot of bodies in class. Naked bodies, fat bodies, skinny bodies, bodies with lumps, bodies with hair. We once drew a lady who had cancer, and she had no breasts, they were removed to stop the cancer, but it still spread, and she died a few weeks after we drew her. She always looked pleased, almost already at peace with what was becoming, what had happened to her. Perhaps she thought that she was saved, by removing her saggy breasts full of cancer, she was now free. But life dug her a hole. And now she was long gone. She was this grand magic trick, of strings and whistles, one minute she stood naked, and I drew around her melted breast plate with my pencil, and the next moment she was candy for the worms.

After drawing class, Tennessee said we should go check out this adult cinema a few blocks from college. Tennessee was this girl in my class that loved drawing tits and nipples, she had sketchbooks full of them. She was half Korean and half Chinese, but she was born in Delaware. She had knife slit eyes and fat filled cheekbones. She always looked the same, a short pink skirt, a shoulder less off-black shirt with frills and crazy eyeliner. Her legs were smooth and even though they were short and stumpy, they were beautiful. The adult cinema had this grandiose entrance with one of those old-time ticket booths at the front, but it was closed. You had to walk inside to buy tickets, which was less fun, but more practical. It was all lit in a dark red hue, and the people working inside were all drained, with satchel faces and smelly armpits. Ten did all the talking, all the dirty men with blubbering guts liked her more than me, she reminded them of their fantasies. She was twenty-one but she looked sixteen. The blob monster behind the counter pulled the tickets out of the machine. He did some last-minute flirting with Ten before she turned around and winked at me. Ten said that Adult Cinema was art-house and held a canvas up to the sexual body, and the patriarchal society, and how it burns and bonks bullet holes into the female form. I thought she looked cute when she was passionate. The film started, and the lights dipped to black all around us, she nuzzled close to my knees, her whole body was aching and itching, right beside mine. I just kept looking forwards at the big screen.

It was a bedroom, but classier. The linen was thin and silky on the bed, and the curtains were thick by the window. The walls were a blood orange and there was a red ottoman by the edge of the bed. The woman walked in, she had ginger hair, and her legs were fantastic. She was Japanese, which Ten whispered into my ear. She was fully nude, and she had a stripe of hair, but it was well groomed and looked tidy. She sat on the ottoman and slowly she spread her legs wide, and she got her hand down below the hairs. As she moaned and rubbed, I looked at Ten. I couldn't see the art-house appeal, but I was getting quite uncomfortably aroused. Ten looked enamoured. She leant over and again caught my ear.

"See the way the red and the orange signifies a woman's blood ritual" she said

I smiled. I hadn't put thought into the colours. I just saw a Japanese girl masturbating on an ottoman with dyed ginger hair. The man eventually joined, he had a suit on at first, with a belt. Ten had lots to say about this. How the belt stood for the stronghold of men, grouped and knotted and tightened together. There was a cult in men, they were strongest together. But notice how easy the lone and exposed woman tears that bond apart, and the man becomes single, and vulnerable, and now she had him, she was in charge from here on out. Or the man was unconscious to whatever was happening outside the windows, but the woman was always hearing and always alive, the man was only alive in his pants, his penis was red, but his mind was blue. A man is better with clothes, she would say, hence the suit, it's an armour, it's a weapon. But naked and gasping for pleasure, that's the man's weakness, that's where he cries and pleads and begs. That's how you destroy men. She looked at me and she said that she liked to be pinned down to the bed, and choked, and how the less she was living the more the man felt powerful, and the more powerful the man, the more precious the woman, the more the man was exposed, the more the man needed, and to be needed was the reason we got naked in the first place. The phallus is always searching for the end. And the woman wants the man screaming, and on his knees, but some women wanted to scream and be on their knees, to toy with the man was fun, to toy with the woman was fun, that's what it's trying to say. I tried to take everything she was saying in, but it was a lot, and she was whispering it, and that made it more tantalising, and I became more turned on, but I held myself together. The man finished on the woman's face and we left the cinema.

"What did you think?" she said

"Interesting"

"I kind of want some now" she licked her lips

"Yeah?"

"You ever slut it up?"

"What?"

"You ever just sleep around?"

"Yeah, sometimes"

"You want to go into the bathrooms"

I stalled and her lipstick was shining as she peered into my soul. The air got heavy, until I tried to reply.

"I...uh..."

"Harper. I'm fucking with you"

"Yeah...I know"

She walked off, her boots squelching with every step. I didn't know if she was really messing or not. I thought about calling Flow, telling her all about Eron, and how I shaved my hair, and how I was slowly killing myself. But I didn't. I wiped the haze from my eyes, and I swallowed my spit. Drifting in front of me, in a pool of milky black water, was a tiny premature tar baby. It's white burning eyes roared at me. It spoke, and the words cut the air like butcher knives.

"What do you want?" the baby cried out

Chapter 22.

Harper's parents had invited me down to the summer house for the week. It was this pretty sky-blue cottage. I was 13. I stayed in this small room just across the way from Harper's. The walls looked ancient and there was this mean smell, kind of like a dead rat. There was a thorny plant on the windowsill, it reminded me of a cactus. There were these expanding fields all around us, and we loved to galivant, and find new treasures in the greens. We found a monster tree by a mouse lake a few days ago. And Harper carved our names onto the bark. This was my last night, and we wanted to find something extra special. We had breakfast with her parents, her mum cooked us some eggs. They were overcooked, and dry, but I gobbled them up fast, I was too pumped for the adventures that awaited. We helped wash our plates and then we set off for the hills. It was a mild day, overcast, and the clouds were covering the sun. Harper led the way, she hopped and stepped over rocks and brambles, her pink wellingtons sprayed some of the dew up and around as she did. At the top of the hill we overlooked some of the fields, they were wide and stretched forever. Harper was goggled-eyed and peered around on her tiptoes, trying to spot the best route, with the most mystery. Her short black and white checked dress blew in the wind. She pointed her fingers and we journeyed onwards. We had to hop over a five barred metal fence, into this farmland. There was a lonely cow tending the meadow, it didn't look up at us.

"You know, if you stare a cow in the face for longer than five minutes, the cow remembers you" said Harper as we walked past it

I looked at the cow and said "Seems happy"
The cow just kept grazing, and we were onto the next field. This one was marshier and muddier, our boots crept through the lush. Harper squelched in the mud, forcing her foot into it, as much as it would go, and then pulling it out slowly, so it would make a big sound. I copied her. We both stood still, sticking our feet in and out, making loud pop sounds each time. The clouds were parting and the sun was finally starting to wake. It melted my face in an amber tone.

"Sun's following us" said Harper, squinting
I could hear this thundering roar from beyond the bushes. I grinned at how stupidly excited Harper became by the sound.

"Maybe it's a storm in the middle of nowhere"

"I don't think that's how storms work"

We pushed past the bushes, and behind them was this huge body of water. Bubbling trickles of waterfalls. The noise was right in our ears. It was sprinkling. The joy on her face made me happy.

"An old stream, must be from the old times" she giggled

"Formed by the god's just for us to find" I joined in

"They wanted us to find it, I'm sure"

We were both laughing, but something about the way she said it, I think she might have somehow believed it, even though I knew she knew it was ridiculous. That was my favourite thing about her, she thought the world was full of magic, that anything could happen, and anything would, and maybe even sometimes, it was meant to happen, just for us. She took off her wellingtons and dipped her skinny toes into the rumbling waters. She waved them about like small fish bubbling to get food. I just watched her. I was wrong. She was right. It was a storm, but it wasn't a real storm, and it wasn't in the middle of nowhere. I had a storm inside me, since I was born, this sort of sickened curse, a darkness. She was the following sun, that calmed it.

"What would happen if I only looked at the cow in the face for four minutes and not five?" I said

"It depends on the cow" she said it so seriously

We stayed by the water until it started to get dark. When we got home the moon had come out, and the lights were all shining inside the rooms of the house. We sat at the table and we ate some leftover pizza from the night before. The cheese was cold and sticky, but it was nice enough. We brushed our teeth together, and then we went off into our separate rooms, across the hall from each other. We left our doors open so we didn't feel too far away. There was this collapsing pit in my chest, I couldn't understand why, but my heart was stinging, and my eyes were wet. I clenched my teeth, and my whole body was warm. I kept looking at the door, and I waited for her to get up and see me and walk into my room. But she never did. A drop of black tar ran down my cheek, like a teardrop. I wiped it off and took a deep and haunted breath. I got the bus early the next morning. And everything seemed different, as if I knew more about the world than I previously did.

Chapter 23.

Welcome to exploding Tom's: Where Tom's explode everywhere. Tom looked up at me and curled his lip slightly. He didn't explode. He was a Tutorial Tom: The Tutorial Tom teaches. He told me about the disaster of 94. How the convenience store (Tom's) was haunted by a strange presence, and how the customers exploded. Tutorial Tom passed me a gun. It was a silver pistol. He told me to watch out for all the Exploding Tom's (which weren't all named Tom, it's just what the game wanted to call everyone). It was a small convenience store, full of fake brand-named products. The gun was fully loaded, and the first Tom appeared out of thin air. This Tom was illuminating blue (she looked like a ghoul, or a ghost) and she was holding a basket of fruit. The music changed and she rushed at me, with the fruit falling out of the basket as she did. I pointed the gun at her face, and I shot. She exploded instantly. Cha-Ching. Coins fell out of her, and I picked them up and I earned some money. The Tutorial Tom popped back up 'Well done, that Tom looked tough, oh and look, she dropped some money. You can use money to buy some cool stuff'. And then he disappeared. The Tom's came in waves, every time getting more difficult to explode. I used the money to buy a purple hat and a better gun. A snot green monster Tom appeared after the tenth wave. He was a big Tom, a very big Tom. The ammo of my new assault rifle was low, and my health bar was even lower. I would have to run about and be tactical here, no time for any funny business, I kept saying to myself. The snot Tom did this thing, he would vanish in a pool of snot on the floor and then dive up in a different spot and swipe at you. I ran around all the produce of the store. I knocked over the coffee machine, kept passing over the spot where new ammo spawned, every five minutes or so I would get a new bullet. I cheaped out on buying the enemy health bar thing, so I had no idea what health the snot had left, I just kept running around, collecting a bullet and shooting. Waiting for him to dive up. Harper was off in college and I was in the arcade at 3pm in the day, fighting a snot Tom. Bang, the snot exploded.

"Nice shot" he said

I pointed my eyes away from a scrambling Tutorial Tom who had popped up, and I saw that Goose had been watching me.

"So many Tom's, so many explosions"

"I bought the purple hat"

"Good choice"

He pulled a cigarette from his pock, like magic. And he danced it 'round the air. He was an idiot, but he knew how to entice me.

We floated high in the sky, perched on the billboard as we watched that same dreary church sit there. He smoked cigs, which were fine, it was nice for a change.

"That game is so stupid" he said

"No. What do you mean?"

"Exploding Tom's! Hello!"

"It's a haunted convenience store"

"Full of exploding ghosts. How do ghosts even explode, aren't ghosts just air and shit?" he smiled

"They are more ghouls than ghosts"

"It's still stupid"

"Shut up. You are just pissed 'cus I can shoot better than you"

"Yeah. Well, whatever"

Goose always had this way about him, this special sort of face, he seemed determined to do something, I just don't think he ever knew what that *thing* was. We understood each other, we had both been through the ringer, I guess. His mum died when he was young, she had cancer. He never liked to talk about it, but he told me about it before, when we were both drunk. He always got sad when he drank. I was always sad when I didn't. That's what separates us.

We would drive all around town, we wanted to discover all the parts of it, even the bits we didn't know. But it wasn't that special, and we had seen it all in a week. We would get drive-through burgers and eat them in his car and listen to music. He liked The Smiths, Pulp and some old rock bands. They would remind me of my dad, he loved all that old rock. We were parked in the carpark of the fast food burger place and *Babies* by Pulp was playing low in the background. I got a chocolate milkshake and I think he got a bag of chips. I kicked my bare feet up. Stars were in the sky, and I counted some of them, but got bored.

"What do you think it feels like to be special?"

"Probably like nothing, right?" he said

He was probably right. I suppled my milkshake and I thought a lot about being someone, like about properly being someone. I don't know why that night stands out for me, nothing really happened different. I guess I just understood something that night. I was a nobody person. I wasn't a somebody. And, it was good to admit that to myself. I pointed my straw at the stars and imagined them all exploding, a whole sky of exploding Tom's, all shining bright.

Goose was hanging his head over the edge of the billboard. A giraffe trying to find food. We climbed down the ladder and at the bottom, I looked up at what it said. It simply said: You are a nobody. I exhaled out of my nose and closed my lips. I gave Goose a nudge on the shoulder.

"I bet we can find a dark cave or somewhere new tonight, what do you think?

"Maybe"

"I think so. I really think we will"

We drove down to the beach, and the sand was freezing cold, but I walked through it with my socks off. And tiny particles stuck to my feet. We bathed our toes in the water, and it made us jump, it was so cold. We chased up and down the shore, falling sometimes to the ground, getting covered in sand. The stars were in the sky again, but I didn't count them this time. I just let them sit there. At the edge of the beach we found a crawling space in the rocks. We slipped through. Goose went first and I followed behind, using my phone's torch to illuminate the darkness. It was small inside, and there was nothing in there but rocks and this slimy green tar. We had found a cave; it was perfect. I switched my torch off. And we both stood in the darkness for a few minutes. We didn't say a single word. I was a nobody beside somebody, in a dark cave at the edge of a beach. And, that wasn't so bad.

Chapter 24.

Diamond worked at a DVD store. They had a clip-on tag that indicated their favourite film: Mood Indigo. A film by French director Michel Gondry, who had a beautiful high-pitched voice, and liked to experiment with abstract stop motion interlaced over live action footage. Mood Indigo had this mouse, which was played by a French actor in a mouse costume with stick on whiskers and a cute plastic tail that he would hold in his hands sometimes. It was this strange love story about a man who falls in love with a women (typical), but then a tiny seed flies into the mouth of the girl and a tree starts growing inside her belly. It's magical. We all watched it at Diamond's house one time, and we were all crying when it finished. Fuck you Michel Gondry, you beautiful French bastard with your squeaky shrill voice. I borrowed his complete works from Diamond. I watched Eternal Sunshine and cried for a whole week. Joel driving back in the car at the end after meeting Clem, and the whole world starts whirling and erasing all around him. I hadn't ever experienced feelings as strong as those ever, it moved me. I watched Microbe et Gasoil after a night out a few weeks ago and forgot to switch on the English subtitles. They built a house car, and it was wonderous to watch. I had no idea what they were saying. Goose came over one night and we both watched The Science of Sleep. The world was made from cardboard, and the main character was falling in love with his new neighbour. But was he dreaming? The neighbour had a fabric puppet horse that she had made, and at the end of the film they both ride the horse into the clouds. And I don't know what it means, but it reminded me of my life.

I met D at *Hail* after me and Harper fell out. It was a place we could be ourselves and not be terrified of what others had to say. I remember it so well. D walked in with a candy red dress and these yellow leather boots. They had streaks of ocean blue in their hair and the rest was a white blonde. I thought they looked magical. D told me their real name was _____ but they preferred Diamond or D.

"I like the white freckles" they smiled

We just gelled instantly. We smoked a lot after the gatherings, and we shared stories and that sort of stuff. I told D about that night at the blue cottage and how that was the first time I knew who I was. D told me about how when they were young, they hated being who they were so much, that they would hurt themselves so badly. They hated how everyone would ask questions, and how people would always say: So, can you explain it to me, I just don't understand? It's all new to me. This is a new thing. D didn't think it was new, they had been living it for years. People always hated what didn't concern them. They ought to mind their own fucking bee's wax and fuck right off back to their badly cooked dinners from their badly dressed, fat and ugly partners. But we didn't care, not really, we were who we were, and we didn't need people to tell us otherwise. We were happy with simply just being.

Goose loved Bad Boys, and D hated him for loving it. But we all watched it together and laughed at Will and Martin making jokes. Even D laughed. G and D got on like fire. We told D about the cave, the dark and stony slit of land at the edge of the beach. D would rarely come adventuring with us. D worked late shifts at the DVD store, it was a 24-hour place. Sometimes we would go and hang with them for a bit, outside the glass panel where you'd have to tell D what film you wanted to rent. We would talk about our adventure that night or about a film or about Harper, and what she might be doing in college. We would talk about lots of things. We went one night after an adventure to the whitest house in town. D was busy with a customer, who was wanting to rent Lethal Weapon 1 and 3. But not 2 or 4. We watched as D handed the customer two DVD boxes. When the customer left, D told us that the customer hated 2 and 4, said they were terrible. D laughed about it. We told D about the whitest house.

"It was very white"

Goose dropped me home that night, and he had a red face on him when I stepped out of the car, he looked nervous, like he was in some rush.

"No fucking way" I pulled on my joint

"Yeap. In the jack's" he looked at his feet

"Tell me everything"

"We both kind of always wanted to"

"And...?"

"Well, D text me..."

"And...?"

"Well, after their shift ended, I drove over..."

"And...!?"

"They make me so happy"

"Ah! OH MY GOD!"

Goose folded a smile on his face, bigger than any he had ever folded before. I was so happy for them both. I pulled on my joint and I thought about Harper. I couldn't wait to see her. She would be home in a week. I had so many things I couldn't wait to tell her. I couldn't wait to hold her in my arms. We made a deal. Don't call, let's just keep living, and when you're back, we can see where we stand. But I didn't need the time. I knew. I always knew. I should have told her long ago. I should have never left that night at the dance. I shouldn't have done a lot of things. I know that now. One more week, and I can see her face again.

Chapter 25.

A rocket punch firework blew up the sky. It rained in spits of red and yellow. I held the back of Ten's head as she hurled green liquid out of her mouth and into the toilet water. She didn't aim well, and her bile was sliding down the white porcelain. I caught myself in the mirror, holding onto her. She was blubbering, and her face looked smacked, but she wasn't hit. The music was loud, but I could still hear the fireworks. I watched some of the colour drop from the bathroom window. She pulled all the juice out of her and she curled up against the tiles of the wall. A chequered nightmare. She sort of laughed, but maybe she was just spluttering. She bent over and slipped off her shoes and folded her toes out. She bent her neck back and leant the crown of her head on the back wall, and her hair tipped into her eyes, but she quickly wiped it back behind her ears. She spat into the toilet bowl and looked out the window as she did. There were translucent bubbles on her teeth from the spit, but she licked them away with her tongue.

"I feel really warm" she said

"Yeah, you're drunk"

"I'm sorry"

"It's fine"

"It's just..." she leant over and spat into the bowl, and continued "Why are you still here?"

"To hold your head"

"We are just two people in a room"

We sat on the bathroom floor, watching the end of the fireworks. The sound of exploding colour drowned, and the music took its place.

"You should go" she wasn't even looking at me, but when she said it, I could feel her breath

"Ten..."

"You don't get it, do you?"

"What?"

"You *make* people like you"

"No, I don't"

"Then tell me, why are you still here?"

"You're my..."

"No" she cut me off, cold and with a sadness

"I didn't do anything"

"You should go" she said

She looked sad, as if her face was breaking. I got up off the floor and I left the room. She didn't even look at me. She must be drunk, I thought to myself, what does that mean, I make people like me, she's out of her mind. I walked into the faces of monsters and drunks. I didn't know anyone, and they didn't know me. We were many people in a room. I left and I went back to my small dorm. I opened the Virgin Mary lunchbox and all that was inside was the handwritten note from Flow, no joints left. I hadn't made Flow like me, had I? Could I do such a thing? No. She kissed me. I couldn't see the fields of flowers, but the moon was in the sky and that looked pretty, so I tried to focus on it. But I kept thinking about what Ten said. Was I really a bad person? I didn't know what was right and what was wrong anymore. I was bald, in a room with no life, and I used Eron, and I ran away from Goose, and I blamed them, I blamed Flow, I blamed Ten, but was I doing it, all that I did, for my own happiness, and not theirs? I sat and looked at the moon, and I kept thinking. I was alone in a room.

The bus pulled up a few minutes later than it was scheduled. I should have been excited, but I was just tired, and drained. I couldn't sleep much. I had this sore headache. I don't know. In a few hours I would be standing across the way from Flow. Like when we were 13 at the blue cottage, across the way from one another. I stayed up all night waiting for her to creep into my room and tell me that she loved me.

But I was stupid. Maybe I didn't make her like me, but I had cheated on her. I left her, and I just really wanted to shine, she always shone, I never did. I was her backup dancer, but I wanted my own victories, my own speeches. I wanted what she had so much. I was playing hopscotch when I first met her, I was drinking out of a juice-box. I used to love juice-boxes. She looked at me then, and I just knew it. I knew it then, and I know it now. I really hate that it's true. She holds me back. She's fire, but she burns. I really hate that it's true. I stood by the bus-stop and I watched the bus leave. We should have slept with our doors closed in the blue cottage. Because nothing should have ever happened, and nothing did. We didn't love each other. We were just friends. She's better off there, and I am better off here. Without each other. It works better that way. I would drag her down, and she would drag me down. I placed the lunchbox on the bus stop seat and walked away. I didn't need it anymore. She wasn't a princess; she was just a girl.

I knocked on her yellow door with sunflowers. It took a few minutes, but I could hear the teether tatter of her feet creeping up to the door, and she opened it. She looked at me, very hungover, but also awkwardly.

"Can I come in?" I said

"Yeah. Sure"

Her room was bigger than mine, and she had a standing lamp in the corner with a green tinge. She was in her pyjamas. She had a mug of tea by her bed, and the quilts were opened, as if she had just got up.

"Do you want tea?" she looked at me

I nodded my head, and sat on the edge of her bed, watching her fill the kettle with water from her bathroom. As the kettle boiled, she stood by it.

"You are right" I said it

"About what?"

"I make people like me"

"I didn't..."

"You did"

"You didn't go home then?"

"No"

"I was very drunk last night Harper"

"You still said it"

"I say so many things"

The kettle steamed and she poured the hot water into the mug. She walked over and sat beside me, handing me the steaming lava. I let it rest on her bedside press.

"I am sorry, if I led you on"

"You didn't, you were just being nice" she said

"I was being too nice"

"Yeah, you were"

"I really want to be two friends in a room"

"We can be…" she took a moment. "Why didn't you go home?"

"There's nobody there for me"

"I thought you said you a had a friend who…"

"She's only a girl, really. That's all"

Steam was still rising from my mug, but I took it into my hands. I felt like I needed something to hold. I don't know why, but I just did.

The lunchbox sat on the bus stop seat for a day or two until finally a young boy stumbled past and decided to nab it up. He took it and opened it. He pulled the note out, in nice handwriting. He read it and crumpled it to the ground. He walked away with the box. The note was left scrunched on the ground. It read: You saved me.

Chapter 26.

A pack of teenage boys had their dicks out, waving them about the air as they pissed on Spongey's gravestone. Yellow dribbles spilled down the carved rock, as they all laughed and spat on the grave. Abigail stood by a small tree a little back from the group with another boy. She was wearing a washed-out grey hoodie and blue jeans. The boy had ash black hair and a yellow jacket. He handed the bottle of vodka to Abigail. She held it cold in her palm, and flipped the thing back into her mouth, and washed her teeth with the liquid before swallowing it quick. She tussled her backpack off the ground and zipped it open. She pulled out a hammer. The piss dripping grave stood there, as the boys all circled 'round, waiting for Abigail. She walked up, slowly, but it wasn't a long walk. She stared at the grave, and she watched the dribble of urine pass down into the mulch underneath. She took the bottle of vodka into her other hand and slugged some. She passed it to one of the boys and gestured that everyone ought to move back. They did. She swung the hammer and cracked the stone slightly, she swung again and again. The stone started to break apart, she kept hitting it until there was a chunk of it smashed open. She dropped the hammer. Her eyes were all puffy, but she kept contained. She grabbed the hammer up and placed it into her backpack and took the vodka in her hands, and they all left the graveyard. One of the boys made a joke and they all laughed, even Abigail.

Mum had this panic room in her bedroom, it was more of a closet space, but it's where she would go when she wanted to cry. I had cuts up my legs, and that was my way out of the pain. Gashes and tears of blood, slices of me, all painted on. I think about him a lot. I was twelve and I didn't know, I thought it was special. I felt like I was needed. I was young and everyone assumed I knew nothing, but I knew a lot, and he knew that, and he treated me like I was older. I hate him for making me love him. My love is dead, and life is worse now. But I get along, for my mother and for my little brother. I am fourteen now, and I still know a lot, but everyone thinks I know nothing, everyone thinks I am broken, but I am pieced together. Not perfectly, but is anyone? I hang around with these group of guys, I just get on with guys better than I do with girls, I don't know why. I feel needed around men. They are all older, eighteen, nineteen.

My body was stretched open on the sand, as he slid in and out and got down on me, and into my mouth, his ass in my eyes. I slopped my spit 'round him, and he jerked it 'round. My teeth softly sparked. He popped out and tore my legs apart, pulling my knees open. He jerked up and down himself before he placed it inside me. He went fast. I watched the terrifying black sky start to sprinkle with a shooting star. As its red-hot tail blew up, I started to cry. He finished inside me, and he pulled out. He looked at my red face full of tears. He crushed his toes into the cold sand and slid his boxer briefs on.

"I am going back to the boys" he said

He left me lying in the sand. I tried to stop myself, but the tears kept running down my cheeks. When I sat up, the whole place was dark, and I couldn't really see too far into the distant. My body started to shake, and my heart was racing. Mummy was wrong. There are no monsters under your bed, they are sleeping next to you, or on top of you, as you scream and shout to get them off. And they are unmoveable, and they bite, and they kick. But the monsters don't have sharp teeth, they don't look too bad at all. They smile and they laugh like you and me. His name was Yellow, because he always wore this yellow rain jacket. He was my boyfriend, I guess. We would have sex, because he said it's what we needed to do, and he said he loved me. I believed it. Yellow had this beautiful smile, and his teeth were white too. He was shorter than average, with skinny arms, but I didn't care. He was nineteen and I was fourteen. He was playing guitar in his jocks, with the yellow jacket hanging over him when I managed to walk back to the campsite.

"There she is" he said

I walked over and sat beside him, and I don't know why but I needed to hold him. I needed something, and you wouldn't understand, he was all I had. What was I to do? I had been pieced together all wrong, and it showed. He sang some Oasis songs, and his voice was all rugged and his hands moved up and down the fret board. Everyone was singing along, and I just watched all the sad mouths flop open, shouting songs into the dark sky. I was on Femondene and my phone pinged telling me it was time to take it. I swung my hand off from around Yellow and walked towards our tent, which was furrowing in the light breeze. I unzipped my backpack and after I took it, I just sat there in the tent, all alone, it was stuffy and hot, and the flapping noise from the wind calmed me. I would have to have sex with him again tonight, and I knew that. If I didn't, he would leave me, and I couldn't be alone, I wasn't able to work by my own. I did what he said, it was easier. I was fourteen and I listened to him.

My therapist glared down at his note pad, which was this small pink book, with a blue butterfly on it. He had big eyes, and a small voice. He was a student therapist, because mum didn't have the money for a proper one.

"Boys can be full on; it's just how they are"
I listened to him, but he had a man's perspective, so he didn't really understand. No man ever could. Not that I told him any of it, I just told him that I was having 'boy troubles'. I didn't want to get into the specifics. I was fourteen and he was twenty-three. And the way he looked at me, was the way every man would look at me. He looked at me as if I knew nothing. But I knew enough. I mouthed in my head. 'Fuck you forever', but he kept talking, that's what they all do, they keep talking. Yellow met me afterwards, we went for coffee and he told me this story about his friend Bobby and how he got with this ballerina last night, and that he had finally lost his v-card, and I smiled and nodded along. Good for Bobby. The ballerina wasn't even given a name in the story, she was a chess piece, she was a statue vagina and that's all they saw of her. A

place to be. Men have this awful problem; they forget their own privileges sometimes. They aren't all bad people, but most of them do bad things. And none of them seem to care. But what do I know, I am only fourteen.

My brother is eleven and he plays guitar. Yellow is teaching him. My mum asks no questions, she sees me with him, and he is older, and she doesn't say anything. I wish she said something. But she is weak and so am I. My brother really likes Yellow, to be honest, everyone does. He is a beautiful person. It isn't his fault that I am glued all wrong. I bring him upstairs to my room, and we slump on my bed. I show him my collection of books, all the stories that I escaped too when I was young. His smile is a hoax that I really want to believe in. I know by his face, that all this conversation, all these jokes and all the laughter is just foreplay, there's a reason he hasn't moved from my bed. There's a reason he is laid down, he isn't tired, even though he says he is. I am fourteen but I am not an idiot. I want to believe so badly that he is, I try and distract him, I show him a book my grandfather gave me, it has pictures of cats. Lots of cats. He smiles at it. But he doesn't move from the bed. The floor is lava now, and I am burning in it. I know what happens next. When I join him on the bed, his smile turns real. No longer a hoax. Men always get what they want. He does all these tells, he slides up next to me, with his crotch close to me, and his legs slightly spread open. You know, as if to give me easy access. Just say what you want. Say it. Just say it. You are using me. You use me. I am fourteen and you are nineteen and you are using me. Please, I need you to be honest with me. I need this. But he knows what happens next too. The next part is easy. We get naked and he gets inside me. And I won't have a name in his stories soon, and that's okay. I have become so accustomed to glaring up at my ceiling. Life is funny.

I dive up and gasp for fresh air. The water is brown, and circles surround my body as I thread the water's top. My arms are skinny, and my fingers are stretched out. The whites of my nails are long, and the green varnish on them is fading. Some of Yellow's friends look at me from the pier, gawking down at me like hungry vultures. Yellow bursts into the water, swims up beside me and grabs and turns me about.

"Do you ever smile?" he splashes at me

I crack my mouth and snap my tongue out at him. I flip him the bird and I dunk his head under the water, but he is stronger than me and turns into my body and wraps his cold fingers 'round my torso. The water is cold on my top half and my lower body is warm.

"I am fourteen" I mouth softly

"What?"

All his friends splash into the water. They are laughing and making boy noises. I slip his hands from my body and I swim to the pier. I place my squelching toes on the ladder and climb up. I grab my towel from the wall, and I cover my body with it. He is staring at me. I smile at him. This evanescent love is nearly over.

The anomaly of his car radio and the way it would infrequently and randomly switch channels, hummed in the backdrop. His friends had all been dropped home when he first looked at me.

"You are acting funny today" he said

"Do you see the way your friends look at me?"

"The guys, they are just guys"

"They look through me"

"You are exaggerating"

He pulled into my driveway, and the bushes were all freshly cut, and the grass was greener than this morning. He turned off the ignition and sighed.

"What do *really* want Abi?"

I couldn't say anything, I just sat in the passenger seat for five minutes, looking out at those green bushes as he kept talking.

"…I think what we have…"

The green was a peeling bathroom green.

"…I have never felt this way about…"

I looked at him as he stopped for breath.

"I don't smile when I am around you"

He looked dead when I said that. I opened the door, and he didn't try and stop me, which was surprising. I stepped out of the car and closed the door shut. I went straight up to my room and I collapsed onto my bed and I glared up at my ceiling. It was unchanged. I was fourteen and I was thinking of ending things again. Maybe I could make my suicide note pretty and draw some flowers on it and maybe even colour them in, and I think I have glitter in the drawer and glue and I could write it in mum's fountain pen, I should buy new ink. People will say I played the victim, those people will probably be men. And they will *get off* to my suicide. I am fourteen, almost fifteen.

Mum jars open the door in the morning, and she sits a mug of hot coffee by the cream carpet. She knows I am unwell. I pretend to be asleep, but she understands, and when she leaves, I bounce up and walk bare on the carpet, grab the mug and slouch on my bed and drink it, slowly. The coffee slumps into my midriff, and outside there is a pitter patter of rain. Why is it that when you break up with someone, they wanna meet up for coffee, because they have 'things they have to say'? Yellow text me last night, saying he needed to talk, and if we could grab a coffee. He still controlled me, even when he didn't anymore.

The coffee place was bright, with low hanging square shaped fluorescent lights. Yellow was sitting waiting as I walked in. He told me that his friend Bobby didn't get with that ballerina, and that Bobby had lied. I nodded my head. Good for the Ballerina.

"I am just afraid you are gonna hurt yourself"
It was his first ever time being concerned.

"You know?" he said

"Never bothered you before?"

"I don't want you cutting yourself because of me" he held my hand as he said it
I pulled my hand away.

"That's not fair" he slid his hand closer
I didn't have anything else to say, so I just sat there and waited for him to speak. I sipped on my coffee, and he sipped on his. We were two people in a coffee shop, like in one of them French films.

"Can we at least still be friends?"

"I don't know"

Yellow convinced me to suck him off in his car after coffee, and nothing really changes, I did it. A sloppy and mouth filled guilt feast. His belly squirmed with joy as I got my small fourteen-year-old lips and teeth up and down him. He finished into my mouth and I cocked the car door open and spat him onto the dirty gravel. I got out, and I started walking towards town. The roads were busy when I got nearer. Yellow drove away to spend time with the boys, and I was alone, with the taste of him still lingering inside my mouth. Why does the fourteen-year-old cross the road? I closed my eyes, and nothing could stop me now.

Chapter 27.

The streets were crawling with faces. Some were more crooked and out of place than others. People counted down in unison. 10. I was cold in that night-time blue. 9. I made my way past a group of teenagers smoking pot out of a pringles can. 8. Goose and Diamond went off to the beach, they hated all of this. 7. I should have gone with them. 6. Why didn't she come back? 5. Nobody really looked happy, even when people smiled, it looked so fake. 4. There's this divine emptiness inside of me. 3. A pair of sneakers are tussled and hanging over an electric wire. 2. There's a place my daddy used to bring me when I was younger, beyond this tired town. It wasn't even pretty, but he used to bring me there, and we used to eat sandwiches and watch butterflies, and he would do impressions of people I knew, and I would laugh at his fat face squishing together as he did them. It was a few months before he died, he brought me up there, and we just talked for hours. About every little thing. I was 13. He was older. I told him about that night at the blue cottage, about my feelings for Harper. I told him I was gay. 1. This is the moment before everything turns black. I know this one too well. Just one moment more. And the whole town went boom. All the lights went dark. Ten more seconds and everything would be back to normal. I just kept walking through the darkness. I was good at it after all.

When the lights flung back on, everyone was holding someone. I was swimming through lovebirds. I was a lonely crow. My legs were machines. The billboard read: Keep going. I got out of the town, and onto the main roads. There weren't many cars. Not really. I had been walking for hours but I couldn't tell. There was a plastic barbie doll by a ditch on the side of the road, when I saw it, I stopped and looked at it. She had curly blonde hair, a sort of skin-tight pink spandex dress, and her boobs were hanging out. They had no nipples. Bald plastic tits. The steaming hot bulbs of the streetlamps shone down like alien beams. The drizzle of rain only appearing in the light. I kept going. I couldn't make out the surroundings so well, but I could imagine them, as I always saw them, driving with dad down this road. I know there's a place with a golden painted metal scarecrow, maybe I have already passed it. It has big bug eyes and a sharp witch nose. I cut away from the main road and onto a smaller side road. I could feel the stones sinking as I stepped over them, dad said 'stones sink 'cus they know they need to', which didn't really make much sense, I think he just liked to say things that sounded all fancy and provocative. He was the sort of man that would burn the manual before he even opened the box. A stubborn mule man, with a round head and moon dimples. An amber flicker ticked in the trees as I got nearer. Trolleys of logs and terrible machinery slept on the tangerine burnt grass. The flicker of the amber light bounced off the metals. There were scaffolding and split in half hard hats, tired old tree trunks and chocolate bar wrappers in the mud. I pushed past the building site, and into the oasis.

Harper held her chin to the window of the train as she watched the sprinkle mist of rain smack against the glass. We were driving into a vortex, an unescapable watery cyclone. At least, that's what it looked like, even though she seemed more interested in the melancholic drift of blurred out tree branches. She was living in that mundane volcano. She loved it in that sad and morose place.

"Where are we going?" she spoke into the glass
"I told you, it's a surprise"
"This is stupid" she sounded serious
"Just wait"

When the train pulled up outside the stop, I could see Harper's intentional glaring daze devour me, but I tried to ignore her sometimes mad ways and told her that she ought to smile more, and to wait and see, that she'd love it. Red leave trees and yellow buildings with pink tiled roofs, it was wonderful. I told her we would have to walk through a field to get there, which she didn't seem too pleased about, but she had no real choice, only to blindly follow me into the storm. I wish I knew how damaging following me into storms would be. Her red boots squelched in the muddy grass. At the edge of the field there was a scarecrow, a metal one with golden paint, it made Harper smile just a little. We were almost there. We pushed on past some burnt tangerine grass and there it was, the oasis. A gloopy and crystal-clear lake. And on the shore, a small lime green paddle boat, for two people.

"You got to be fucking kidding me?" she said

"You'll love it"

"I'm not getting in that... thing"

She was such a stubborn cow sometimes, but I knew she was hurting. It was two weeks after the incident, and I could see that she had this burning linger in her eyes. It was fresh and unsaturated. I sat beside her, and we watched the ripples of the lake for a few moments.

I was translucent around her, she made me this intangible thing that I could hardly understand.

"Dad used to bring me out here a lot"

"I'm not doing it" she coldly snapped

I stood up and trudged towards the boat and I pushed it into the water, and I climbed up, and inside. My socks and shoes were soaked wet, and the lower parts of my jeans. But it was worth it. Harper was a blot of paint on the tinged grass as I paddled out to sea. I didn't go too far out, I just wanted to show her off, I wanted her to care, I dunno. She just sat there.

"You happy?" she looked at my wet sneakers

"Why are you such a dick?" I stared at her

"What's this all about?"

"I just, I thought it would be fun"

"It's stupid"

"I was just trying..."

I know it sounds so mad, but I wanted her more than the stars want the night to fall, more than whales need water, more than a laughter needs a smiling mouth. I wanted her, and by the look in her damned eyes, she wanted me too.

The lake was invisible in the night, but when I stood up to my knees in the water in the dark, I knew it was there. And that's all I wanted, to know that it was there. I will go on and be the same person I was today tomorrow, and the day after, and it will all start to bleed into itself and become this purulent period blood colour. I will become that blot of paint. But the truth is simply that we will all become mere smudges of colour, non-existent marvels, only visible by the eye and only said to be alive in the world, by the people telling the story. I found the boat, peeling and tired, piled in sand. I flung my body out from the water. I cupped my fingers together and started shovelling the sand from the boat. Heavy gestured motions. The breeze blew leftwards, and the sand sprayed away from me, taken by the blow of the wind. Flying particles in the air. I could start to see the wooden seats of the boat, a washed lime green, a rotten wood consistency. I had most of the sand off and I started to push the boat down to the shore, I was pushing an elephant into bath water. The body was massive, and heavy and intense. I kept pushing the dirty elephant, it was bath time after all. Its feet smashed into the water, and I caught my breath. I climbed into the boat and I struck my hands into the water and paddled furiously out into the ether of black. If only my dad could see me now. If only Harper could see me now. The crush of cold water trembled under the boat's wooden bottom.

The inky water fizzed and popped. I took a joint out from my pocket, and I lit it. The waves crushed up and wet the papers. The ember still flamed. I counted down. 10. What the hell was I doing in the middle of this black lake all alone? 9. I can't even think properly anymore. 8. I should have never told her that I love her. 7. His face was a steel blue when I walked in on him hanging, he looked so empty. I remember it like it just happened. I closed my eyes and I was there in that room with him. 6. I feel a part of some sort of fantasia, is that normal? 5. I am so afraid. 4. I get it now, the stones sink, because they have to. 3. This water is so cold. 2. I miss the billboard. I miss when I was younger. It just went, a crackling bulb that danced so beautiful. 1. This is the moment before everything turns black. I paddled and I paddled further and further into nonsense land. And I closed my eyes, took one last pull and I jumped from the wooden thing and into the coldness. The black tar dragged my body underneath. It was pitch black, and then suddenly, from the bottom of the lake. Two white lights. They were eyes and I was in the body of a creature. It all seemed so real.

Chapter 28.

I looked so silly. I never wore platformed shoes and I couldn't even walk in them properly, but Ten said they looked nice and that I needed to make an impression on the public. It was the end of the schoolyear and the big showcase of all our art. We all had to have a theme, and I chose *The Naked Female Body: Against a World of Bleeding Fields*. Breasts and bodies in a red landscape of roses and poppies. It was a white walled room and everyone had their own place on the wall to display, I had four paintings, and Dominika Romansky was to my left, and she had all these beautiful charcoal drawings on the darkness of light and how they both can't exist without one another. Ten was a little away from me, her collection was beautifully and elegantly titled *Areola and the Dust Cloud inside my Bellybutton*. She drew tits and stomachs, all in these vivid paints, they were perfect. The doors opened and people started to shuffle through, my parents were coming up for the day, and I was anxious about that, so I was a bit more on edge than I usually would have been. School faculty were the first ones inside, and they gazed about, eyes on the paintings and pictures, humming and hawing as they went, not knowing how exactly they should react to drawings of mostly nude forms and odd hellish voids. But they all smiled at me once they looked at my paintings, which was hopeful. Misses Lumen stopped and took a doddered look at the seas of red and the breasted women lying inside of them. She swaddled her eyes on one of a black girl lying in a bleeding field of roses. She spoke so gently, with an almost whistle in her vocal cords.

"What does it mean to be there?" she said
"In the field?" I wondered
"Hmmm"
"It's a representation. The blood colours, the nakedness. In that place, it's a woman swimming in her own bleeding mess. She is scared, of herself. But she is safe in that place too, it reminds her of the people that she once loved, it's a fantastic place, almost dreamy. It's period blood, but premade. It's all parts of a woman, and flowers, and it's there, and it's here."
"It's really nice"
She smiled and she shook away from me and my corner. I took a breath. A few more heads went around, none of them stopped at me for too long, and barely any of them said a word. My art teacher, the Swedish chef, came around and smiled, but he had

seen the paintings hundreds of times, so he didn't stop, but he was nice to me, so I didn't mind. He knew I hated this show-off thing.

It had been 2 hours and we had another thirty minutes left. Eron walked into the room, he looked skinnier, he had more of a defined jawline, and he looked good. He walked up to my paintings and looked deep at them; his eyes were so big.

"These are really good" he said

"You didn't have to come"

That made him smile, and he looked so good when he smiled.

"Are you wearing heels?" he laughed

"Shut up"

"You're not really here, are you?"

"I am right here"

"But not really, I mean, this isn't you is it?"

"I am still unchanged"

"I don't get you Harper"

"You don't really know me"

"No. I guess I never really did"

He turned away and didn't look back.

"Those are really good though"

He walked away and just left me there. I was still just me; I have no idea what he was on about.

Mum and dad walked through the door, and swung their arms around me, and mum cried, and dad tried so badly not too, but I think a droplet fell out. They looked at my paintings, and they seemed so happy and so proud and I couldn't understand it really, I wish I knew what that was. But I didn't. Dad left to walk around and see all the other art, mum stayed with me.

"When I was your age, I was very sick. I don't think I ever told you that. But I nearly died."
I didn't know what to say to that.

"But I didn't" she said

"I don't know what to say"

"Your dad would never tell you this. But when I was dying, on that hospital bed, he was there every day. And if it wasn't for him being there, I might not have made it, and if I hadn't made it. You wouldn't be here"

"That's a lot"

"I am terribly proud of you"

"Thank you, mum"

"Your nan's earrings"
I was wearing the blue earrings.

"You look like her today"

"I feel lost"

"Do you want to know a secret?"

"Yeah"

"I do too"

Dad came back, and mum smiled at him. She really loved him; it was special.

"They are all so talented" dad tried to explain

It's weird, my parents were strangers to me in that moment. It's as if my imaginary friend had finally come alive. I only ever known them to be imaginary, and now that they were real, they seemed so different.

I stood nude in a field of bloody white daisies. The artist lives inside of the art, every brushstroke. The sky was dull, and the field didn't sway, it was ever so still, almost unmoveable. The blood was mine. I thought a lot about what my mum said, about her being sick, about how she is lost too. All my family were dangling from the trees in the distant. My grandfather smiled at me, as his neck snapped. I wish I could explain why I painted this one, but I can't remember. I wish I still had that Virgin Mary lunchbox; I could kill for a smoke right now. I wonder if the *me* in this painting dies when I do. And why was I naked, why is everything naked. Art is always naked. I could look good in clothes. I hate this painting. There are so many feet walking over my body right now.

Plying my chest open, scavengers, vultures. People just come and go, in and out, ghosts on acid. The difference between me and her was that she fought her way out of everything, I just ran from it all. When you are young nobody ever tells you that life is fucked, you watch cartoons about bears with hearts, and you play on your bike and everything is rainbows and sunshine. If everything was so perfect, explain to me why I have become this naked painting. Why I am half girl and half devil. I want to shoot love out from my chest, that's what the bears would do. But none of it works. You grow up too fast, and then cartoons seem stupid. True love's first kiss, true love's first fuck, true love's first orgasm, true love's first strap on, true love's first fuck up, true love's first abortion, true love's first cut, true love's first orgy, true love's first house fire, true love's first decapitation, true love's first world war, true love's first death, true love's first mass suicide, true love's first sex trafficking, true love's first period, true love's first school shooting. And what about true love's last kiss? It's all too much. I miss the billboard, I miss being young and hazy, unaware of the storm. I am a girl in the middle of it. It's up to you now. That's what they say, right?

Chapter 29.

A girl on acid. Hands wavering over the sea-puss. Jellyfish lapidifying and sinking under the crust of the ocean floor. The hilarity of the half goldfish, poking its head, it's tail, the other half in a different place doing a dance, two parts, two halved, one fish. What's that movie with that one girl who get molested by Robin Williams called? Even clowns are vilified. My bathwater is lucid blue, and my feet are sexy (?), I twirl them up to look at my ankle, the ankle might be the sexiest place on a human body, but it gets lost under a thick sock. Ankle socks save the sexy place. I grab my phone off the dipped corner of the bath, it's soggy from all the moisture but I grasp it in my cold fingers and slob water on the screen as I type my code: 4556. I look sexy right now, I think to myself as I click into the camera app. I take a picture of my ankle; I want to remember this later. I think about sending a nude to someone, the thrill of my body on someone else's mind, my nakedness in water, my tits on T.V. I think it's called *Insomnia*. What did Eron mean when he said, 'You are not here, are you?'. What does that even mean?

I submerge out from the lucidness gloop of blue water and stand in the bathtub. I bend my back over and pull up the towel (which is a hand-towel, as I couldn't find a bigger one anywhere (what are bigger towels called? (Bath towels))). I am a body standing in a body of water. The mirror reflects a dire story. My tits are unchanged, I should warn you, one is bigger than the other, if you were to see them, you would notice, and I know that's normal, but mine are circus tits. I wipe myself dry, starting from my face. Then my arms, and around my shoulders. I get my chest, then my torso. Over and around my back is next. Then I step out and onto one of those cushioned things that are in bathrooms, a bathmat. I think that's what they are called. I do my legs, they are smooth, I just shaved them. They are pretty legs. My feet are last. I can now see my face much clearer in the long-standing mirror. My hair looks like the peach fuzz of an adolescent boy. I have this urge to let go, but I can't help but hold on, does anyone else feel like this? I used to have this blog called 'How to safely self-harm' it got a lot of views, and all those people existed, or still do, or have died. Countless little children, or older, or younger, I don't know their exact ages, but nevertheless, all people. Blog reading, self-inflicting people. A collective of no goers, of all doers, of sheep people with personal torturing thrills. They have names too. And sexy ankles. I wish I reached out more, but sometimes I feel like holding on, but I can't help but let go, do people feel this too? I am reading a book at the moment about a girl in a bathroom, she is naked, and afraid, and she doesn't know what to do. But what happens next? I wonder if she's going to be okay.

The encumbered street whore plays wallyball with her local pastor. He is a thick black man with shoes on, and the general pastor attire. The boy cycles his bike past, the sun stroked yellowness whimpers, as if the sun has a date soon, and wants all the people to hurry the fuck up. It disappears behind a cloud in some sort of *ex abundante cautela*. It means what it means. The boy is nearly home, but a few miles remain. White line, gap, white line, gap, the roads love games. Fat men are driving smaller cars lately. One of them picks his nose before fingering his blonde girlfriend caked in pumpkin coloured fake tan, she moans, it's a good finger fuck, proper long fingernails too. The wheels of the bike screech as the boy heads down a thin alleyway. There are no people, just him and the bike. It's a narrow street, the gap between the thighs of an anorexic sixteen-year-old who pukes out her dinner are bigger. He stops up outside a small house. His mum smokes a big cigarette and smacks his plump bottom, not in a sexual way, but in a gesturing of, you are my son and here is me smacking your bum, to say, hey you, you are mine and you popped out of my hu haw. A gentle smacking, a maternal slapping, a hand on ass love clap. The boy walks inside and turns on the T.V. His mum walks in.

"I cleaned that thing for you" she says
"It's pretty cool, right?"
"It's blasphemous and wrong all over"
"It's funny"
"It's on the dishrack, drying out"

The boy gets up and walks into the kitchen. The adverts turn to the programming and that plays lowly in the background. It's a re-run of a late-night talk show. Some children's T.V actor blabs about their new cancer film, but the boy doesn't pay much attention. The boy spots the lunchbox shining in the pale pink sun, Virgin Mary's eyes looking at him. The boy is right, it is funny.

Ten's place looked barren without all her stuff in it. The dorm room was a shell now. An empty place. I tied the knot on the last bin-bag and tossed it by the door next to all the others. Ten looked sombre, she knew that the year was up.

"Home will be nice" I tried

"Nice. Yeah, I guess so"

"Look's so different"

"As if nothing ever happened here"

"Illusionary happenings"

"So, you are really going to stay here?"

"Yeap"

"It's not a place to spend your Summer"

"I just like it, being here"

"What about home?"

"Home is there, always will be"

"Harper, nobody is waiting for you here"

"Exactly"

"This is an underworld"

"It's a college dorm"

"Not here, there" she pointed on my chest

Chapter 30.

She was right, this was no place for Summer, these badly painted walls of long narrow corridors with small windows, what was I to do here? I was to do everything or nothing. That's what she said before she left me. I remember a time less lonely, when I was younger, but it's too blurry to be fully painted. I prophesise a downfall, a pomegranate sways on a tree somewhere, as they say.

We are all gathered here today to celebrate the funeral of Harper Goodview. (Celebrate?) She was a girl on acid, she lived too close to the sun, much like those who came before her, and those who will fall after she has been fed to the rats. Eron is there, he is fat again, he must have put on weight since I saw him last. He sits next to his wife, is it his wife, it could be his daughter. Tennessee is there, she is alone. She looks different, tamed, as if the phase of being herself ended. Goose stands by the back wall of the church with D. I haven't seen them both in so long. I miss them. They seem stone faced. They are standing so far from my coffin. I don't want to know if she's here. So, I stop looking. I let the priest do the thing. And God will take this one too, as they have done before. God is still real in this future. The voice of the priest and of my inner self have merged into one, I am the priest and the priest is me. This future has no meaning for you, but it exists and thus it goes on, he says, or do I? I continue, and so does he. But don't let that mess with time, it's never minding and understanding, and nobody ever really knows anything really, if you truly think of it, but still there are some with stroke faces, let time stray from those with faces of strokes, they are unclean, unhailed, polished up all wrong, with a dirty cloth, sliding skin, maybe they care, possibly caring, too much, possible, but time can't think, it never would, if it could. Ding dong, and God's at your door, they brought some strudel, a welcoming gift, or a parting gift, but it's your strudel now, and you better like strudel, because God has made you some, and it would be rude not to eat God's strudel. Holy strudel tastes good even if you hate it. Do you invite God in for tea? Does God drink tea? Or is God more into coffee? God is like time, it does not think, it does not do, it just spreads itself over an imaginary and uncontrolled axis. The God axis. The boy who stole the lunchbox has not attended the funeral, that boy had no knowledge of the people involved in said funeral, so no blame nor guilt is taken.

Her parents, my parents, have died before me, before her. Cancer of the neck, strangled by a rope, drowned in a vat of pure unfiltered chemical acid. They were parents on acid. In the end, they were too, parents in acid. Irony of time, of God, of parents, and of acid. Please be seated for the prayers of Saint Clooney. Do you think it's going how you/I expected/wanted? It's not bad, I/you suppose. In the name of the (God's) father, the (God's father's) son, and the Holy Spirit (?), it so be, or it is so. It's time, he says to me, or I say to him. But time has no purpose I say, to myself. He says I must stop saying I and start saying we. We agree that this course of pronouns work. We have run out of time and of God. The Happy Reaper appears, why would death's taker be grim when their job is to take. Maybe they dislike their job as many do. They reap what was sown, we the girl and the priest of acid must be drained into that other place, that everyone keeps banging on about. We close all eyes.

"I knew her when we were kids" she says
Who is that speaking? We remember that voice so well.

"We used to sit on that billboard just outside of here, I still can't believe people still use it. Maybe we were stupid to get so close. We loved…"
Why does this speech not continue? Or has it just

stalled. Is the voice thinking, or are they crying? I don't want to know.

"I miss those days very much" she says

"We are drowning" we speak

"One of us anyways"

"You'll be better off without us"

"You don't understand, do you?"

"We were never meant to be born"

"Harper, listen to me"

"Mum was sick, she should have died"

"I don't have long left"

"We know, we will be gone soon"

"You are all that's on my mind"

"We should come back"

"You made me bloom"

"We were just young"

"You destroyed me"

"We had no idea"

"Something happened me Harper"

"Are you ready to tell us?"

"It was the middle of the night"

"We should have been there"

"It was a child's room, full of toys"

"We were all children"

"I told him to stop"

"We never asked questions"

"I wanted to kill him"

"You should have told us"

"I followed him; I saw red"

"What are you talking about?"

"He was sitting in his car with this other girl"

"Flow, what are you talking about?"

"I watched as he died"

"We don't have much time left"

"You never listened to me"

"We loved you, how could you say that?"

"It's funny, this feels so calm"

"What does?"

"It's almost over"

"Wait for us"

"I waited all my life"

"We should have never left"

"But, you did, and you never came back"

"We shaved our head"

"It looks like peach fuzz"

"It's growing back slowly"

"Can I tell you something stupid?"

"You can tell us anything"

"Remember the blue cottage?"

"In the middle of nowhere"

"I waited all night, with the door open for you"

"It was so cold"

"I thought you'd walk through the door"

"We wanted to"

"But you never did"

"All the lights go out soon"

"Just for a few seconds, right?"

"Right"

"Harper?"

"Yeah"

"I am sorry we never worked"

"There's still some time left"

"You were sipping your juice-box"

The crush of waves echoed through the church.

"What's that?"

"It's water, can you not feel it?" she says

"Why water?"

"I told you, I am drowning"

The tangerine light refracts off the bathroom mirror. In my room, the paintings of blood are stacked in piles by the door. I notice the fields are covered in water, the blood has washed out and the girls are sinking. I wonder why I painted them, and why they are changing. My room hangs high in the sky. The birds fly by, as I stand in all my nakedness. The walls have fallen apart, and the clouds have shifted into my room. Down below I can see the church. My room has become the billboard. On the railing, just like new, sits the Virgin Mary lunchbox. I walk out and I open it, and inside there's one simple joint. Before I can think, a lighter appears in my hand, how did this get there? I find myself smoking, in my room, the new billboard. If I jumped in a dream, would it really kill me? The faucets in my bathroom exploded, and water started spraying all over the floors, I didn't notice until it was too far gone, and water filled my bedroom floor, slowly I was being taken by the waves. I watched it happen, and I smoked that joint so tenderly.

"You will have to jump" says the joint

"There's still time" I keep smoking it

In times like this, I wish I had done more with my stupid little life.

"Me too" says the joint

The water had reached my knees, my sexy ankles had been taken from me, and so were my feet. My paintings were swirling underwater and my Radiohead vinyl's, and my everything.

So, you want to know how to safely self-harm? It's rather simple really. No need for needles, or scissors or blades or knives or 8mm pistols. Let me tell you what worked best for me. I met her when I was younger, she told me 'that we were friends now'. I lived through her and she lived through me, we were transcending transparency. Mum didn't think I'd ever find a friend, so she was belated by the thought of it. Flow and I, we lived it all, every miniscule motherfucking minute. It was tough when her dad died, she changed, I never said that to her, but when he went, a part of her did too. She got in so many fights. I was cutting myself, she knew about it, I told her once, but we would barely talk about it, it was easier to pretend the shitty things weren't happening. What's the point crying over spilt milk? I kissed her, and she ran away. She kissed me, and I ran away. And the funny thing about it all, the tragic and messed up truth, is that I have never felt like myself without her. And I wanted to be alone and happy, I mean, I wanted to know what that was, so I left because I thought that's what you had to do. But I feel further from myself than I ever did, I have no idea who I am anymore. And it's cheesy and melodramatic and nonsensical and it's just about a girl who loves another girl, that's all it ever was, but now what, what happens next? So, there's no need to scratch up your arms, all you really need to do, is to fall in love and wait, because it will hurt. I promise.

The water was now at my neck, and the joint was singing a final tune.

"You've taken my legs, knocked me right
down. Beautiful haunting perfume cloud"
This water is unlike other water, the texture is heavier, almost slimy, as if it is some hellish creature eating away at my sallow skin.

"And fools rush in, but they too wash out,
And how do we know, when it's time to let go"
I placed the embered wand on the lip of a golden ashtray. It stood up and it kept singing.

"It's all a lie
and nothing's true
a voice at my funeral
spoken too soon
watching it end
umbrellas explode in the wind
But what's left now?
Shave your genitals
suicide loves
her hands as paddles
You get on the bus
It's almost here
Please wait for us

I am coming dear"

My phone started ringing underwater. I dived down and the screen was all glitchy, I couldn't see who it was. I surfaced, with the water gushing over and back. I answered, but the voice was all muffled, my phone was soaked in water and it was stammering and fizzing uncontrollably. The phone stopped working. I froze and out from the window, all the flowers were growing. And millions of premature tar babies crawled up the stems. One of them stopped and its eyes widened, big white moon eyes.

"You never came back" it spat out

Ink rained down and formed and fused with its body. It was growing, bigger and bigger. I swam towards the corner of the room, away from the beast. Its white eyes shone on me like beaming headlights.

"What are you?" I yelled out

It ripped the roof off the building. We were high in the sky, and its monster ink fingers pulsated above my body. It glared down at me.

"I must be dreaming" it slowly started to melt

The black tar sprayed down and splashed against the water. It smashed against my body and my face. I was covered in thick black ink. I washed my face in the water and the beast was a baby once more. It stood on the edge of the billboard.

"I am sorry for living" and it jumped
The ink and the water vanished, and I was standing
still in my room, as it had been before all this madness.
My phone started ringing. I picked it up.

"Hello" I spoke so slowly

"Harper…" his voice sounded so broken

"Goose" I knew what he was going to say

"It's Flow. She's missing"

Chapter 31.

The school corridors were freezing cold. Everyone was out looking for Flow, she had run off. It was our first teen disco, she looked so gorgeous, she had sparkling yellow eyeshadow on, and her eyes were white stars shining in a black night sky. She got into a fight, which wasn't anything surprising, but she really got angry this time, there was this fever in her eyes. I didn't know where she went, and I was worried. I searched everywhere, but then I remembered the one place that nobody would ever think of, the place she would never ever go. School. It was still open, they had sports games in the gym at night, and the school did admin work after hours. It was bleak in there, late at night, echoing and wild. Every step I took, the noise of my boots hitting the floor resounded 'round and bounced off all the walls. I wish she didn't listen to everything everyone ever said to her, maybe then she wouldn't have to fight as much. Where would she go? I kept thinking as I walked those hallways. I was always searching for her, even when I wasn't. She was always there, in my head, on my mind, escaping me yet again. I nudged further into the school and found myself in the cafeteria. It was still the same as ever, bland and uninteresting. But it was empty, which was a different sight to behold. I took a mental scan 'round to see if she was hiding anywhere in plain sight, but that wasn't really Flow's vibe. She was mysterious and hard to understand. I have no idea, why out of everyone in that playground, that first day of school, why she picked me. I was playing hopscotch and drinking my juice-box. Maybe she liked that I kept to myself. Nobody understands the pain of being a child, it's crippling, and terrifying. But she made it easier, she made everything easier. If only I could stop losing her, then she'd be perfect. The guy called her a 'monkey whore' and said, 'your daddy killed himself to get away from you'. She punched hard, and wild, and crazy, and spat at him, and tore his shirt, and kicked him, and scratched him, and he punched her in the face. She was fire, but he was big, and he was heavy, and he punched hard. Her face rippled, and blood sprung from her mouth, and her nose crunched in, and I think it's broken. She ran away. He just laughed, they all laughed at her.

The sound waves of my boots trampling down the halls screamed forwards. The void of bound things leapt into my ears, and I could hear a new noise. Flow.

I left my head and rumbled into the girl's bathrooms. It was empty, and the noise seemed still. I called out.

"Flow, is that you?"

The bathroom had an even clearer echo. I wondered was I just hearing things, an ear way oasis? I checked the stalls, and one was closed, I knocked on the door and I waited for a reply.

"Flow, it's me, please open the door"

She was always stubborn; she didn't say a word. I knocked again, this time with more fervour and more strength.

"Flow, please"

My cheeks became red and my body started to hurl upwards. I was angry.

"Flow, talk to me"

I took my foot and bashed against the stall door. It banged furiously. I kept kicking at it. But it just kept banging back and forth. I needed a moment to catch my breath. I poured open the faucet of the tap closest to me and washed my hands, I don't know why, they weren't dirty, I just needed to do something. She was impossible, and she knew it. I was never going to win. I sat on the ledge of the sink and waited.

"You have to come out sometime"

The bathrooms were painted this intense pink as if to

remind us that we were of the womanly kind. Why was pink a woman's colour? What's so maternal about pink? I kept my eyes on the stall.

"How's your nose?"

She didn't reply, of course.

"The disco sucked. They really think that's music. It's just random noises really, that's all"

Nothing, not even a peep.

"He's an idiot"

The stall was unchanged.

"Flow, you are…"

I noticed a stream of blood seeping under the stall and I rushed over to see. I banged hard against the door. And again. And again. I searched 'round the room, and I saw the fire hydrant. I grabbed it and bashed the door, as hard as I could. And the door flung open. I dropped the hydrant and I fell to the floor. Her phone was covered in blood, my blog 'How to Safely Self-Harm' was open on the screen. I screamed the loudest I could. The tonsils in the back of my throat burnt up, and my vision was all blurry. Flow's hands were sliced up and bleeding, I held my palms over the big gashes and tried to stop the blood. I screamed again. After a few moments, the principal rushed in. He grabbed his phone out from his pocket and rang for an ambulance.

His words were mumbles as I swam in the whites of her eyes. They were spilt milk lakes on a night sky. She was a dying flower, and I didn't know how to save her.

I stood with the principal as the ambulance drove off. The flares of red and blue burnt our skin. He looked pale; I had never seen him look so real. He put his hand on my shoulder.

"It's going to be okay" he softly said

He didn't really treat us the same after the incident. I guess he understood us more, I think when you see someone bleed, you understand why they bite a little harder. I went home and I deleted my blog. I did this to her; I made her the way she is. I know it. That should have been me, in that bathroom stall. That should have been my blood, and not hers. I should have walked into her room that night, I should have kissed her on the lips and told her that she was the only thing that kept me living.

Chapter 32.

Her body had been missing for two full days. It was bursting down in rain, the rainiest week in years. I was wearing Flow's pale green raincoat and Diamond and Goose were both with me, we all looked like ghosts wandering mulch fields. The haunting dew flicked off the flowers as we passed through them. The flowers yawned as they were sleeping, they were dying without the sun, they needed it, and it showed. We marched through marsh lands, our boots filled with mud and our eyes blurring from the lack of sleep. We trudged through the old cornfields, it was midnight and we all had torches. The weather was at war with us, and the chaos of water splashed off the corn as we pushed further into the abyss. We came to an old red barn, and Diamond and Goose pushed the doors open enough for me to squeeze inside. They waited outside while I crept 'round. My torch was low on batteries, so it kept flickering on and off. I stood in the middle of that barn and I took a breath, I needed one. It was empty, and she wasn't anywhere to be found. The water smashing against the windows reminded me of a water cyclone. I knocked on the door and Goose and

Diamond held it back open for me. I squeezed out.

"I think I know where she is" I said

That golden scarecrow still looked the exact same. She took me here after she tried to kill herself, and I was angry at her, and I was mad at myself. I was so cold to her, but I wanted her more than anything. We found ourselves at the oasis. The lake water was tar black and it crashed against the sand. It seemed empty.

"What is this place?" Diamond said

"Flow called it the oasis"

"Harper, are you okay?" said Goose

I could their voices, but I couldn't see them anymore. My torch was dry and blew its bulb. The waves crushed against the shoreline and thousands and thousands of tiny premature babies crawled up the sand. They were washed ashore from the waves. They moved like spiders, fast and haunting. They dashed past my feet and surrounded the whole beach. The ocean was made of tar. I soaked my body and swam inside of it. The tar entangled me. I was being dragged down underwater. My body was useless. It was so calm underneath. It was a serene nothingness.

"Harper, can you hear me?" she said

"Flow..."

"Harper" they screamed out

I awoke on the beach gasping for air. Goose and Diamond were knelt over me, holding my body.

"What happened?" I cried

"You jumped into the water"

I watched the waves. They seemed so calm.

It must have been 4am on the third day, we were all eating burgers in Goose's truck. Parked in the parking lot of the greasy fast food hole. My face was washed out, big red circles under my eyes, and night looked merely like day, only darker.

"She's got to be out there somewhere" Goose spoke from a spell of silence

"We'll find her" said D, holding Goose's hand

The rain pelted the truck's roof, and I opened the door.

"I am going to get some air" I said

The fake lit bulbs blew white noisy light out under the car park. I looked up at the rain, and my face became wet fast. I wiped it dry with my sleeve, and I walked towards the fast food windows. There was an orange tinge light inside, and it was practically empty, except for a couple sharing a large fry. They were about sixteen, and considering the time, had most definitely snuck out, they smiled and laughed. I walked into the fast food joint, and their whispering laughter became the only noise in that place, as the front of house worker mopped the floors.

"I'll be with you in just a sec" she said

I looked up at the menu, not sure why I had walked in. She plunged the mop head into the bucket strainer and squeezed. And slowly made her way 'round the counter and smiled at me.

"So, what can I get ya?" she said

I looked over at the two sixteen-year olds laughing, and then back at the worker, who seemed strangely unmoved. She still had this smile on her face, she was good at her job.

"Can I have one strawberry milkshake"

"One strawberry snow blast shake?"

"Yeah, what did I say?"

"You said milkshake"

"What's the difference?"

"One's a milkshake"

"And what's the other one?"

"A blast shake"

"Made with milk?"

"Yeah"

"One of those please"

She went over to the milkshake (blast shake) machine and started mixing (blasting) my shake.

I slumped back into the truck and suppled at

my shake. It tasted very blasted. It was freezing.

"You know this is called a blast shake and not a milk shake, even though it's made of milk" I said

"But that makes no sense" said D

"They blast it" said Goose

I looked out at the rain, and I laughed, for the first time in three days. For the first time in a long time.

"Is it my fault? I asked

"It's nobody's fault" said Goose

"I should have come back"

"Yeah, maybe"

"I wanted to"

"Then why didn't you?"

I sucked hard on my shake.

"Harper, you're a good person" he said

I ran off on him, I used him, I did everything someone could do wrong to him. How could he still think that I was a good person? I burst out crying and I couldn't contain myself. I was wailing. Goose opened his door and climbed into the backseat. He held me close to his chest, in the middle of the rain, in the middle of that grease stained fast food hole. In the middle of the storm.

"I put you through hell"

"You were hurting"

"I keep doing bad things"

"Harper, that's all everyone does"

"I love her"

"I know you do, and she loves you too"

"Goose, I am so scared"

He clenched me harder, and I knew then that he was crying. The wilderness of the weather was twirling into corruptive visual light glitches and burning winds. The lights in the fast food place jolted on and off, and the two sixteen-year olds started dancing in the light show. Screaming laughing. I took Goose's hands and we danced to the thundering blows, to the disasters, to the wickedness.

Late that night, a small boat crew found her body. The storm was her way of saying goodbye, we just didn't know it at the time. All the lights had gone out and this time none of them were turning back on.

Chapter 33.

I stood at the edge of Flow's front room, my head just underneath a portrait of her and her dad, which I painted after he died. Her coffin was in the middle and people passed in and out looking at it, humming and hawing, not sure of how to act. A futile art exhibition. A toucan shaped clock, weirdly too colourful and ridiculous for a funeral of a 20-year-old girl, ticked loudly through the quiet room. I am sorry for your loss, for your loss, your loss, loss. Loss, the word, it started to sound fake the more bobbing heads that said it. Budding thespians all reciting the same prescribed monologue. Every hour the toucan would toot and yell, which made everyone very awkward. I thought Flow would have found it funny, so I actually liked hearing that terrible bird squawk, and it was nice to see all these boring ghosts bubble up with fear of reacting poorly to this bird clock interrupting this young girl's funeral. It's all one big show, her dead body was the main attraction, arranged so purposefully in that wooden box, ornament white pillows and silk sheets. 'She looks so beautiful' people would say, as if she was walking down the catwalk wearing the latest trend setting fashion piece. She looked beautiful when she was alive too, but nobody compliments the living. I wanted the stream of 'sorry mouths' to end so I could be alone in the room with her, but they just kept bobbing along. I refused to shake hands with anyone, Flow wouldn't have wanted me to play the game, so I didn't, I told them all the same thing.

"You shouldn't be here"

Hours and hours passed, four or five toucan screams later, and the room was empty. No more fake plastic sentiments. I was alone in the room with her. I was now sitting on one of her kitchen chairs, wooden and tacky looking. Still underneath the portrait. I found myself unable to move closer to the coffin. I took a juice-box out from my pocket, I had been keeping it for this moment, I know she hated them, but deep down, I know she would want me to have it.

"A big turnout. It was nice. The clock kept screaming, and cawing, everybody got so nervous. You should have seen some people's faces. I have been underneath the portrait I painted after your dad died. People kept looking at it, they would all say, 'it's so sad', which I guess it is…that's all they kept saying. It's all…"

I wiped my face with my shirt, my lower lip was spread apart, and it kept jittering around, making it hard for me to speak.

"...Gone"

I held my head down, and the tears ran 'cross my cheeks in streams. I couldn't even tell if I was crying, but I was, and I couldn't seem to stop. Goose walked into the room and pulled a chair up beside me, he looked pale, from the length of the drudgery and from all the crying.

"Did you hear that woman saying Jesus must be in the toucan?" he slightly laughed

I smiled through the tears, but it didn't stay long.

"This is..." I tried

"Yeah" he understood

The rain was still smashing off the windows, and I altered my eyes from the window to the floor, every few seconds.

"She never wanted you to come back" he said

I looked up from the floor and at his face.

"She was so proud of you"

My lip was trembling.

"We found this cave, at the edge of the beach, we tried to search every inch of the town, we wanted to explore everything, we wanted to find something unfound. Something we could carve our name onto. Something that could be ours. It was slimy, full of green tar, and it was terribly small, and dark and wet, but it was…it was ours"

"It's okay" I said, knowing it was not
I held him, and he held me. And the toucan yelled, and we both looked at the clock. It wasn't on the hour, it was out of time, it was all wrong. It was Flow, she was telling us that everything was going to be okay. It's weird, but the toucan almost sounded like it was crying, even though the noise was the same racket as always, for some reason, this time, it just sounded different.

Everybody stood there with umbrellas, as the rain pelted down. I was standing with my peach fuzz out, letting the water devour me. This next part hurts. Her coffin slowly fell into wonderland. But maybe Flow was just dreaming. Like Alice, with the wonderful white rabbit running late.

"Happy non birthday" they would sing
And she would be sitting at the long table eating cake. And the mad hatter would be surprised, because he would soon learn, that she was madder than him.

My mum drove me home, after the show was over. It was dark and the rain had simmered, the storm left when she did. What if the weather was people, forgotten and tired old people, trying to tell us all something, but none of us listen, none of us know to listen?

"It's been a long day" she said

"I feel so lost"

I slid my head onto the glass.

"I have something I want to show you"

The car drove slowly through the night, the bumps on the road shook my face on the glass. The echo of the moonshine refracted off the streetlamps. The lights blurred into a line, a singular beautiful line that I could trace with my pinkie. The stars were clear and bright. After some time, the car pulled up and mum put it into park. She opened her door and looked back at me.

"Come on" and she got out

I sat there for a moment; no lights left to trace. I took a breath; it had been a long day. I opened my door and I stood out of the car. It was the old church, where Flow used to hang out. The colour of light flashed and lamps of green, purple, orange and yellow illuminated the church. The place looked done up, and the sign was new, it read: HAIL, for Flow.

"It's only small but..." she said

"No. It's beautiful"

"It's a place for people to heal"

"You?"

"When I was sick, yeah"

"You tried to?"

"I was hurting"

"Mum"

"Yeah?"

"Me too"

Chapter 34.

When I was a kid, I would see ghosts following me around. Green whisks of smoke. They were particles of energy whirling 'round thin air. They wouldn't scare me; they were my friends. Sometimes I miss seeing those green phantoms, those impossibilities of light. I dream about the ghost of a girl I once knew following me around. White tipex freckles on her face. Grief is a ghost too, it follows me. I want it to touch me and for it to cure me, but it never gets close enough.

It's strange being in my old room, the walls all look so familiar, the paint, the light sweeping from underneath the window curtains, it's a harsh yellow streak of light. I swear one day my life will make sense. I make that promise to myself in my old bed, as I stare at the yellow light. I get to my feet, and my soles are cold on the wooden floor as I walk over to the curtains, towards the stroke of light. I pull the curtains back and bask in the shining. The world is plastic. I forget to breath, but I keep going. I will keep going. I make that promise as I walk to my bathroom, for my morning piss. Another stroke of yellow light.

I get out of the car, and my mum walks up to

the door of the Hail church. Wiggles the big key around and opens the heavy doors. We have a few minutes before people start arriving, if anyone even shows up. I look at mum.

"When I was younger, I could see ghosts"

"Green whisks of light, right?"

"Yeah, how do you know?"

"You told us about it"

"They followed me everywhere"

"It was just your mind Harper"

"And then they just left"

"Everything leaves"

A truck pulls up, and he steps out.

"You didn't think you were doing this without me?" says Goose, walking towards the door

"Goose" I swing my arms around him

Soon a few cars start arriving, all these kids have lost their ghosts, and they are looking for something more. Strange and broken half people. New ghosts.

We are all sitting around in a circle, there's seven kids, and I understand every one of them. It's my time to speak and I start:

"My name is Harper. When I was younger, I could see ghosts, these strange green lights. They followed me everywhere. But they left. And I was so alone. But then I met her. She was more than a girl, more than a ghost. She was a princess. And for a moment, a small singular defining moment, she was mine and I was hers. I just want to feel real again. I ran away, I thought that's what you do, but now I know. I was her ghost, and I left. I left her all alone. And now she's gone. And I can never get her back. If you can, try and hold on to your ghosts, and if they disappear, just know that you are not alone"

Going around that circle, learning about everyone, it was beautiful. I had found a purpose. Something I was searching for.

On lunch break Goose insisted we go for a drive to get burgers. The roads were quiet, and the low humming radio was playing, as usual. I noticed we weren't driving to where we normally would get burgers. We were driving on these steep off roads, that were leading almost nowhere. Into the wind.

"Where are we going?"

"You'll see" he said

We arrived at this pebbly beach. Goose turned the radio off and looked at me.

"Come on" he said

He got out of the car and I followed. It was blue and the wind was battling against our bodies, blowing like an eagle. He started walking down the pebbles and onto the sand. It was that hard-soggy sand, so it was easy to walk on. The cliffs were carved by giants, that's how the fable goes.

"This is the middle of nowhere"

"No. It's the middle of somewhere" he smiled
He led me towards the edge of the cliff and stood waiting for me to catch up. There was a slit in the stone, a small opening.

"I needed you to see it"
I slid my body through the small gap and into the cavern, it was tiny just like Goose had described it. It was pitch black. I held my hands out and touched the cold stone all around me, thinking how Flow had been here, and had touched the same walls. This green tar was new and held no semblance to the black tar of the babies. I wondered what it was, and where it had come from. Suddenly a light illuminated the cave and moved along the walls. Spills of light. Outside the cavern Goose was holding two flashlights. I noticed the flashlights in the car, but I didn't say anything. He was sweet, I shouldn't have run away that night at the drive in, I shouldn't have treated him so badly. I yelled out.

"The ghosts, I can the see the ghosts"

Even though I knew it was fake, I believed it for a moment. It offered me this escape, this nuanced feeling of home. The lights disappeared and I crawled through the slit in the rocks and out to Goose. I flung my arms around him once more; the wind howled against our bodies and tossed our clothes around in ripples and our hair furrowed into our faces. What if the green tar was leftover ghost? I wanted so badly to believe in something spectacular.

When we got to the church, it was well past lunch, and I noticed a girl sitting by a tree in the distant. I told Goose that I would follow him in. I watched the girl as I sat in the car. She looked so familiar, yet I had never seen her before. I swiped my hands around the car drawer and found a pack of cigarettes and a lighter. I got out and walked over to the girl. I lit one of the cigarettes and started smoking it.

"Do you want one?"
She reached out her hand and I handed her a cigarette and she placed it on her lower lip, and I lit it.

"I was just at the beach, there's this cave"
She didn't say anything, I'm not sure if she was even listening. She reminded me so much of myself.

"I lost a friend a few weeks ago"

She had a pale face and a red nose.

"It's a beautiful plastic nightmare"

She held the cig in her fingers, and she flopped her lower lip down and held her words a moment before speaking.

"I am sorry about your friend" she said

It was nice to hear her voice.

"Can I tell you something?" she said

"Anything"

"When I was younger, I could see ghosts"

I smiled; she was the splitting image of me.

"Then they disappeared?" I softly recounted

"Yeah, left me all alone"

She suckled back on the cig and I watched her, she was a broken piece of glass, you could see it in her eyes.

"I am Harper, by the way"

She put the cig in her fingers once more and looked down at her feet, which she kept moving around.

"Abigail"

I knew her pain, I could feel it multiply within my bones. All tawny and inky.

"I used to see ghosts too Abigail. But they were a fiction, a source of my pain. But there's real ghosts too, people who will love you, trust me"

"I crossed the road, to see what was on the other side" she said

"Do you want to know a secret?"

"Yeah"

"It's all the same, every side"

"What are we supposed to do?"

"Survive. We must find new ghosts"

I always hoped I was special, I think deep down we all wish that, but I am just another person in this place that nobody understands. I am a ghost wandering into the night sky. I am my nakedness in a field of red roses. I am half girl and half something else. I am midnight and I am sunset. I am completely and utterly lost.

I stood in my room and at the box that my dad gave me for my birthday all those years ago. With nan's earrings, I put them on. I was meeting Goose and Diamond for a smoke. And god knows I needed it. It was a terribly dark night, more pitch black than usual. I looked at that red dress hanging in my press, the dress I wore when I first kissed her. I slipped it on, and I headed out. I met them at the bottom of the billboard. I hadn't been up there since she left. Goose said he had a surprise for me, but when I looked up at the billboard all that it said was 'better beer today, and even better prices'. He smiled and shook his head.

"Not the board" and handed me a shoe box
I opened the lid and inside was a metal tin lunchbox.
It had a painted picture of Flow on it, dancing, with
her tongue out, she had her white freckles, and she
looked so happy.

"Fuck you" I grabbed him so hard
We climbed that ladder and made it to the top. All three
of us sat and looked out at our world. A small broken
town, but ours. I opened the tin and inside were these
beautifully premade joints. Just like Flow used to have.
I took one out and into my fingers and I sparked it. I
took a big puff and passed it 'round. I noticed a note
inside the box, folded up. I took it out and read it.

"No way" I said putting the note back
"Harper, this isn't for you" he said
"I can't"
"Just think about it"
"Flow would want me here"
"It's not about her...and no she wouldn't"
"What about all those kids?"
"They don't need you"
"I need them...I need you"
"Just think about it"

The note read: Now it's time for you to leave. We
smoked another two joints and then we climbed down

the ladder and back to reality. The smog of real life.
Diamond held my shoulder.

"Something happened to Flow. I don't know if she was well. There's so much madness. And, it's okay to be scared, and it's okay to be what you want to be, to do what you want to do. Don't let fear stop you"

"Thank you" I held in my tears
They kissed Goose on the lips, and went down the midnight roads, into darkness. Goose looked at me, and his eyes were big and bold.

"How are you two doing?" I said

"It's mad how someone else can make you feel"

"Yeah, don't lose that feeling"

"I'll try not to"
I took a deep breath.

"You will visit me. And write?" I said

"And call. Always"

"Look after the kids. They are special"

"I know. I will. I promise"

"You mean so much to me"
I stood back and I looked up at that towering billboard.
He held my hand.

"I never noticed how ugly this thing was"
He laughed and squeezed my hand more.

"Goose, can you do me a favour?"

"Yeah, anything"

Mum was standing at the door, she was smoking a cig, and she looked happy. Goose waited in the car as I stood beside her.

"Are you okay?" I looked at her

"Yeah" she held me close

She let go, and she smiled at me. She wasn't just my mum; she was my friend. I turned away and I opened the car door. I sat on Goose's ravaged passenger seat. He didn't have the penis shaped air freshener anymore. People grow up and they change. He opened his lips and he spoke.

"Stones sink 'cus they know they need to, Flow told me that, I didn't understand it, but I think I do now" he held my hand "Shall we?"

"Yeah" I smiled

He started the car and I knew then that the life I once knew, was ending. *Pink Glove* by Pulp was playing loud as the trees blurred and the wind screamed. We stopped by a set of lights and the premature tar baby crawled 'cross the white and black striped crossing. It was older now, more grown, but it had ways to go, it had more roads to cross, but it was blooming. Just like me.

"Did you do me that favour?"

"Yeah, of course" he smiled

The lights turned green, and green means go. The inky tar baby flung it's arms 'round the tree and tried to climb, it pulled its body up, and up and up.

Goose parked up the truck. He cocked the door and opened the boot. He handed me a box, and he took the other. Just two this time, no need to bring the world, and anyways, I wouldn't be here forever, this wasn't home. We trudged up the stairs, and when we got to the top, Ten was standing waiting by my door. She had a flamingo dress and big hooped earrings, and her hair was dyed pitch black with a white stripe hanging through it. Goose placed the box on my bed. He held me in his arms.

"Are you sure you don't want to stay?"

"No. I should get home. D is waiting"

"Promise you'll call"

"Promise" he smiled

He stood by the door and he laughed.

"You know, you left before the film ended that night. Were you ever curious to what happened?"

"She married the boy?"

"No. It was never about the boy"

"Then who was is about?"

Goose pointed at me and he smiled.

"It was a really good film"

"I am sorry I missed it"

He took one last look around, and then he left. Ten rushed in and choked my body in her arms.

"I missed you" she said

"Ten. Never stop being you"

"Where did that come from?"

"Just needed to say it"

"I'll try"

She was holding me, looking at the boxes on my bed.

"Cool bird" she said

I looked around and I saw the toucan clock sitting in the box on my bed. Goose, you beautiful bastard.

I stood at the bottom of the billboard, peering up at its looming beauty. A few of the kids from Hail, the ghosts of gone off kids, stood beside me. I held the metal tin lunchbox in my hands. It had a picture of a girl on it, she looked like fire, a radiant and flaming fire. Goose had given it to me, and he told me about this place. He said Harper wanted me to have it. We all climbed the ladder and when we got to the top, I popped open the lunchbox and inside were these perfectly pre-rolled joints. A dinky pink lighter, and a small crumpled up note. I took a golden stick in my fingers, and I lit it up in rainbows. I unfolded the note, and then I passed the joint 'round. I held the note in my hands, and I looked down at the church, at all the shuffling people getting into their cars. This was our world now. We had been lost for so long, but now, we had found new ghosts. The moon was hanging in the sky, but it looked different. I squinted my eyes and for a moment, it looked like there were two moons. They looked like eyes, glaring down from the darkness. Suddenly a splatter of black ink spilled from the sky and onto the note in my hands. I squished my fingers in the ink and wiped it away. Underneath it revealed the handwritten message, it simply read: Beware.

Author's Note:

I started writing this book in June 2020 in the middle of a global pandemic and at the cusp of what would become the worst mental health period of my life. I had no idea what this book would even become, It's weird, it's as if this book wrote itself and I was the fingers that touched the buttons. But, I think it turned out rather hopeful, in that it's a story of passing the torch, yanno, it's about growing up really, and I wanted to be true to that, and to show how grey that can sometimes be.

There is an inky darkness that exists in all of us, waiting to bubble up to the top and burst right out of our mouths and ears. I think somewhere in my mind, this fizzling ink baby creation, was born out of my trauma and pain. My mind became the monster, and I think that's what inevitably succumbs Flow. Her mind is her enemy, and I think we all face that in some way or another. But of course, it's best left sorta open, I think maybe we all have something that we must beware of, if it's hurting us or saving us, maybe we all have different places to sorta visit and explore.

You probably don't care about this page.

During the making of this book I drank over 500 cups of tea. I also switched from cow milk to oat milk. I started writing this book in Cork, Ireland, but finished it in Pori, Finland. Other places I wrote parts of this book include : The train from Helsinki to Oulu, Amsterdam airport at 4am in the morning and outside my back garden in the breaking sunlight.

I would like to thank the following people:

Maeve, for bringing me along to Finland, and drinking wine late at night in the Finnish cold.

Dillon, for listening to the rough cuts of chapters from the book as I wrote them and for always encouraging me to keep going.

Megan, for making me believe that I am a flower princess. For helping me grow, and see worth in myself.

My family for putting up with my declining mental state, my crippling meltdowns and for helping me to become the person I am today, you are my ghosts, that I will never leave behind.

And to you, in all your damaged glory, thank you.

If you enjoyed this book please give it a rating and review on GOODREADS and AMAZON.

CPSIA information can be obtained
at www.ICGtesting.com
Printed in the USA
LVHW021709200121
676999LV00010B/1800